DOPPLER

ERLEND LOE is a Norwegian novelist. His eight books have been translated into over twenty languages.

DON BARTLETT lives in Norfolk, and is the translator of, among others, Per Petterson and Jo Nesbø.

DON SHAW lives in Denmark and is the compiler of the standard Danish-Thai dictionaries. They have previously collaborated on novels by Roy Jacobsen and Jakob Ejersbo.

DOPPLER

by

ERLEND LOE

Translated by Don Bartlett and Don Shaw

First published in the UK in 2012 by Head of Zeus Ltd.

Copyright © Erlend Loe, 2004
Copyright © Cappelen Damm AS, 2004
Translation © Don Bartlett and Don Shaw, 2012

Published in agreement with Rogers, Coleridge & Whte Ltd. 20 Powis Mews,
London NW11 1JN, in association with Cappelen Damm AS, Akersgata
47/49, Oslo, Norway

9 7 5 3 1 2 4 6 8

A CIP catalogue record for this book is available from
the British Library.

ISBN (HB): 9781781851050
ISBN (eBook): 9781781851128

Printed in Germany.

Head of Zeus Ltd
Clerkenwell House,
45-47 Clerkenwell Green,
London EC1R 0HT

www.headofzeus.com

november

The woods are lovely, dark and deep.
But I have promises to keep,
And miles to go before I sleep,
And miles to go before I sleep.

ROBERT FROST

My father is dead.
    And yesterday I took the life of an elk.

What can I say?

It was either her or me. I was starving. I'm beginning to get quite thin, I really am. The night before, I was down in the Maridalen district of Oslo and helped myself to some hay from one of the farms. I cut open one of the bales with my knife and filled my rucksack. Then I slept for a bit, and at daybreak I went down to the ravine east of camp and spread out the hay as bait in a place I had long considered perfect for an ambush. Afterwards I lay on the side of the ravine and waited for several hours. I knew there were elk here. I'd seen them. They've even been right up by the tent. They lumber around here on the ridge apparently following their own rational impulses. Always on the move, elk are. They seem to think all other pastures are greener. And perhaps they're right. Anyway, in the end one came along. With its calf tagging behind. That put me off a bit, that did, the calf being there. I would have preferred it if it hadn't been there. But it was. And the wind was coming from just the right direction. I put the knife in my mouth, not the little one, the big one, the big knife, and waited. The two elk were ambling slowly towards me. Nibbling at the heather and some of the young birch trees down in the ravine. And at last there it stood. Right beneath me. A hell of a size. Elk are big. It's easy to forget how big they are. I leaped onto its back. Of course I had rehearsed the routine in my head dozens of times before. I had anticipated that she wasn't going to like it and would try to get away. And I was right. But before she managed to get any speed up, I had driven the knife down into its head. With one mighty thrust the knife had gone right through the elk's skull and into its brain, from which it stuck out like a slightly odd hat. I jumped off and crawled to safety on a large rock while the elk saw its life flashing before its eyes: all the good days of plentiful food, the lazy, hazy, days of summer, the brief love affair with the bull during the autumn breeding season and the subsequent loneliness. The birth and the joy of having passed on the genes, but also the taxing winter months of earlier years, and the restlessness, that unsettled force from which, for all I know, she may have considered it a relief to be delivered. She went through all this in a few short seconds before she dropped.

I stood watching her for a while, and her calf, which had not run away but was now standing beside her dead mother, not totally aware of what had happened. I felt a pang of something unpleasant, something alien. Even though I'd lived out here for quite a while this was the first time I'd killed, and now I had killed a large animal, perhaps the biggest in Norway and, contrary to all my good intentions, I had brutally exploited nature and probably taken out more than I could put back in, at least in the short term, and I did not like that. There should be a kind of balance in things. Hunger is hunger, though, and I would have to give something back later, I thought, jumping down from the rock and chasing away the calf before I pulled the knife out of the skull and slit open the dead elk. Piles of intestines spilled out and I sliced myself a bit of the belly and ate it raw. There and then. Like a Red Indian. Next I hacked what I could into manageable pieces and carried some of them up to the tent, where I collected the axe and went back to chop up the rest. By the evening I had transported the whole of the animal to camp. I fried large chunks of meat on the fire and ate my fill for the first time in several weeks. I hung the rest of the meat to smoke in a primitive kiln I had spent the previous days building. Then I went to sleep.

And when I awoke today, I heard the calf outside my tent. I can still hear it. I hardly dare get up. I can't look it in the eye.

I can't stay lying here, though. I need some milk. Skimmed milk. I don't function well if I don't have any milk. I get irritable and I'm quick-tempered. And I know very well that I'll have to go down amongst people for some milk. That's why I'm reluctant to go, but I simply have to have some milk. Occasionally I do go down to Ullevål Stadium like any normal man. I used to do it a lot more before, I know, every

5

day in fact, but after I, well, how can I put it, after I moved into the forest, for that is actually what happened, that's what I do, I live in the forest, since then I have been there less and less often. One of the reasons is that I don't have any money. Another is that I don't wish to meet people. They disgust me. Increasingly so. But I must have milk. My father also drank milk. But now he's dead.

I can still hear the calf outside the tent. It's actively and noisily reproaching me. It's trying to psych me out. But I burrow even further down my sleeping bag and tie up the top so that there's like a gap between me and the rest of the world. I can't get out and the world cannot come in and I'm lying there as quiet as a mouse, like a child, pretending nothing has happened for quite some time. But the calf won't give in. It just stands there, and stands there. And then I have to go for a piss. My God, it's just a calf, I tell myself. Why should I, a grown man, have a bad conscience about killing an elk? It's nature's way. The calf will have to learn, and it should be happy that it's me, Doppler, who is teaching it and not some more unscrupulous individual who might have made cold meat of the calf as well while he was at it.

I go outside for a piss. Same place as always. On the flat rock below the tent. From there I can usually see the whole town and the fjord, but not now because it's misty. And I completely ignore the calf. I simply pretend it doesn't exist. It's wary and watches me pissing. I try standing with my back to it, but it must have caught a glimpse of me and wants to see more. It moves and watches from a new angle. I turn away but the calf follows me. It's as if it wants to make sure it wasn't seeing things. Like everyone else. The story of my life. OK, OK, for Christ's sake, I say, and turn to it with my trousers around my knees and my arms in the air. Have an eyeful, I say. Feel better now? Have you seen enough? Satisfied?

But the cheeky little bugger's not satisfied. It keeps staring. And there are limits to the shit I can put up with from elk. I grab the axe lodged in a nearby tree and hurl it with all my might at the calf. It leaps to the side and runs off between the trees.

Life's taught me that I come off badly if I try to hide the truth, so I may as well give it to you straight: I have a big member.

What can I say?

I have a remarkable, indeed an extremely large, organ.

In short, a gigantic chopper.

I always have had. It is large. There's no better word for it. It's long and it's heavy. And fat. Hence, large.

At school they called me Chopper Doppler.

Fortunately, that's many years ago now. It's not something I think much about any more. But it was hurtful. After all, I did have other qualities I wanted people to see.

Chopper Doppler.

Actually, it is very annoying to be reminded of it. I hadn't thought about it for ages. That bloody elk. If it comes back, I'll split its skull open.

 7

There was no milk for me yesterday. I spent all day hunting that damned calf. Of course it came back fairly soon after I had chased it into the forest. And to my great annoyance it hung around for hours on end outside my tent. Not unlike the pupils at Sogn Secondary School beneath me here – which looks as if it was designed with the purpose of relieving some Gulag. I've cycled past it for years. And now I can see it through the binoculars if I can be bothered and if there isn't any mist. The pupils usually stand on the street corners hanging about in a pathetic, ungainly way while smoking as much as they can before the school bell rings. If the calf could get hold of cigarettes, it wouldn't think twice about starting to smoke. It's all alone and it's beginning to realise the world is a harsh place, and it cannot see any future or meaning in anything. Of course, it's immature of it to take out its frustration on me, but what else can you expect? After all, it's only a child.

After a while I'd had enough, child or no child. I quietly put on my hunting gear and charged out of the tent with raised axe ready to strike, but the little sod got away again. And for many hours I hunted it all over the place up here. We went along Vettakollen Ridge, down by Lake Sognsvann and even almost the whole way up to the high Ullevålseter meadows. The GPS showed that we had covered almost fifty kilometres at an average speed of twelve kilometres an hour. In the forest and over mountainous terrain. It was dark before I returned to the tent, absolutely exhausted. And, when the calf turned up shortly afterwards, I had run out of steam. I gave up. We slept together in the tent that night. The calf supplied a surprising amount of heat. I used it as a pillow for most of the night, and when I woke up this morning, we lay looking at each other in a close, intimate way that I had seldom experienced with people. I don't think I've ever experienced this with my wife. Not even at the start of the relationship. It was almost too much. I apologised for killing its mother and said that it didn't need to be frightened any longer and that from now on it could come and go as it pleased.

The calf, naturally enough, said nothing. It just looked at me with its big trusting eyes.

It's fantastic being with someone who can't speak.

Yesterday we spent the whole day in the tent chatting. I gave the calf some water and fetched it some branches with succulent bark on while frying myself large chunks of meat in the embers of the fire. As I groomed its coat with my comb, I explained, in pedagogical manner, that while humans had hunted elk for thousands of years, it wasn't for fun but borne of simple necessity. And if the elk stock had been allowed to multiply uncurbed it would have had catastrophic consequences, I said, without quite knowing what I was talking about, but I thought I had heard or read about this somewhere, so that's why I said it, and I said that when there are too many elk, then they spread diseases, mental as well as physical, and in the end what you get is a really unpleasant atmosphere in the forest. Just imagine it, I told the calf, who by the way ought to have had a name, I'll have to find it one, but I told it to imagine the situation: row upon row of plague-ridden, mentally ill elk fighting over food and running around in all directions mooing and bellowing, breaking the laws of the forest and elk etiquette in a most degrading manner. No one wants that. That was why my forefathers hunted elk, and that's why we hunt elk today, I said. Even though today we don't need their meat or skins to survive, I added in an undertone, we still do it. We think it's good fun to go into the forest and shoot elk. There's a feeling of camaraderie between the hunters, I've learned, I said, and that has become a custom. It's force of habit. And, furthermore, to keep the numbers down, as I've already mentioned. So that's how it is. But I didn't kill your mother from force of habit. I did it out of need. I hadn't eaten for days, and besides I hadn't had a full stomach since the blueberry season finished. And I'm sorry I did it with a knife, I said. That was unnecessarily brutal, but I haven't got a gun, and I can't shoot, either. And I do understand it if you feel resentful and are caught between emotional extremes in your relationship with me, I said. That's okay with me. You'll have to examine your feelings and draw the line wherever you think. But I want you to know that I'm ready to support you in these difficult times, I said, and by the way, I continued after a short pause, your mother would soon have brutally broken the ties between you two in any case. She would have shoved you away from her and told you to push off. Because that's the way elk are. You lot seem so good-natured, but you treat your kids like shit. You're bestial. You give birth to kids and give them milk and a helping hand and then whoosh, just as the kids are feeling snug and out of harm's way, they're given the heave-ho. Before long, maybe even next week, your mother would have insisted you go your way and she hers, and it would have been a sorry day for you, a day most elk never get over, but now you're spared that experience because I did her in, and instead of remembering her as someone who spoke with a forked tongue, you'll remember her now as someone who was always there for you and who was suddenly and meaninglessly whisked away, I said, grooming its coat with my comb.

Incidentally, I also lost someone not so long ago, I went on. I lost my father. I hardly knew him. I never knew who he was. And now he's gone. So in a way we're in the same boat. You've lost your mother and I've lost my father. And instead of directing your anger at me, you should direct it at Herr Düsseldorf down in Planetveien. For a long time I had easy access to food in his cellar, I explained. His late wife used to make enough jam from berries to last me a lifetime, and not only that he's got a well-stocked freezer full of bacon and other types of meat, and after studying the neighbourhood closely for several weeks I discovered that Düsseldorf's house was the easiest to break into, and that Düsseldorf made it even easier by being inattentive and generally lethargic and

11

also somewhat given to drink, so in the evenings while he was sitting there engrossed in his stupid war models, always Second World War vehicles, which he made on a 1/20 scale or whatever, paying all too much attention to detail of course, and to giving them the correct colours, I entered the house by the back door which was wide open all summer, and went down to the cellar where I unashamedly helped myself to the goodies, into my sack with them and out I went again, through the garden and back to the forest. This was an arrangement which I found to be perfectly satisfactory for both Herr Düsseldorf and me. You see, he's got everything he needs in this world. Big house, a stock of food, plenty of money according to the bank statements on his bureau next to the cellar door, and on top of that a hobby which apparently fulfils and enriches his life. It's difficult to imagine what more Herr Düsseldorf could wish for, I told the calf. It was almost as if I had begun to believe that if I rang his bell and asked him straight out if it was okay for me to break into his house once in a while and freely partake of the surplus in his cellar that he would smile and say yes. But then he must have changed his mind, for one day not so long ago the back door was locked and a sign and stickers had been put up about alarms, security guards, crime and punishment. That's what the world has come to. People brick themselves up and are frightened of each other.

So I was left high and dry and as the days passed I began, as is only natural, to get hungry. And I just got hungrier and hungrier and in the end I could see no other way out, I had to lure your mother into an ambush and stick that large knife of mine in her skull. That's what hunger does to you. Nothing else matters. You just have to have food, I said to the calf. Maybe you've experienced something similar yourself, maybe not. Let's hope not.

The need for milk has become acute and I stuff fifteen to twenty kilos of elk-meat in the sack and make my way down to Ullevål Stadium. The calf trots after me, but in a stern voice I tell it that's not on. You'll have to wait here, I say. Wait, I repeat with conviction, as if talking to a slow-witted child. I'm unshaven and scruffy and look conspicuous enough without your help, so I don't want to have an elk straggling behind me. Don't worry, I say, I won't be long. But it does worry. It doesn't want me to go. Poor little elk, I say, you think I'm going to abandon you, but I won't. I just have to go to the shop and get some milk and a few other things I need. This has no effect. Separation anxiety shines out of its eyes, and it concerns me that it is so clingy. I thought elk were more independent. It's attaching itself to me in a way I'm not sure I'm ready for yet. I catch myself blaming its dead mother for taking the calf with her on a walk, slap bang in the middle of the hunting season. What was she thinking of?

I stop, put down my sack and cuddle the elk. Try to lift it up, but it's too heavy, so instead I massage its head with my knuckles in a playful, affectionate way. I give it knuckle, as we

13

say in my family. Afterwards I explain the situation in an unhurried, orderly fashion. I'm a great believer in explaining things. I've always done that with my children too. Children can sense that there's something up if you lie or withhold facts, I tell myself. Therefore I explain, using body language, that I'm going down among people and it's much too dangerous for a little elk. There are cars and buses down there, and lots of noise and all sorts of confusing signals. In fact, that's the most distinctive feature of humans, I say, they're the masters when it comes to confusing signals, no one can match them, you can search for a thousand years, but you won't find more confusing signals than those that come from humans.

And when elk happen to stray among humans they're shot, I say, miming a stray elk being shot and dying a gruesome death. So, I say, it's best for you to wait here. I'll be back in a couple of hours, then we can get together and do something nice.

I wait for a sign that it's understood me and that it agrees, but it's not forthcoming. And despite all my explaining and all my kind intentions it still follows me. In the end I tie it to a tree. That settles that.

The manager at ICA is dubious. I can read him like a book. The doubt oozes from every pore. Help a poor old hunter-gatherer, I say, but I can see he thinks it's weird.

We're standing in the stockroom and he's trying to put on

a stoic attitude, but despite all the smiling training and theories about how the customer is king, he radiates scepticism. What I'm asking is, of course, way beyond all the rules and regulations. I offer him elk meat in exchange for milk and a handful of other wares from his rich assortment, and he doesn't like it. I know that most people think that this type of economy is a throwback, I say, but here I am anyway, and the meat is good, and besides it's an excellent economic system. You barter. You do things for other people. I'm sure it's on its way back, I say. It's coming back, and if you go along with this you can boast later that you were ahead of your time. You were a trendsetter because it's absolutely certain that bartering is coming back. In ten years' time bartering will be the norm. It's obvious, I say. Things can't go on the way they are doing now. It's no good. Open virtually any paper or magazine and you will see that nowadays there are hardly any discerning people who are in any doubt about how we have to change our consumer ways if we're going to keep things going for more than a few decades. And I see that's your view too, I say. You're a thinker. I notice you haven't said no.

He's in his mid-thirties and actually pretty pleased with himself. It's quite clear that he's well-trained, for a shopkeeper, and thinks it's exciting to be involved in building up ICA at Ullevål Stadium. The shop has been done up and everything. One of the country's most modern supermarkets. Refrigerated counters as far as the eye can see, including, incidentally,

Parma hams costing thousands of kroner, cheeses as big as houses and no doubt a great work environment where people matter to each other and are committed to their workplace. And he's in a quandary. He's got a lot to lose, but what are the chances of anyone finding out, and anyway he likes elk meat. In a way, there's no arguing with elk.

He looks around to make sure none of his staff is close enough to take note of what he's going to say. What are you after? he says.

I say I'm after several items, but the most important thing is to set up a milk deal. A milk deal? he says. I nod. I, that is, my organs and cells, in short, my body, need a good litre of skimmed milk a day, I say. Therefore I'd like to find, every Monday and Thursday morning, when the shop opens at seven, three and four cartons respectively of skimmed milk placed outside the stockroom, for example between the waste skip and the wall.

Why skimmed milk of all things? he asks.

My good man, I say, skimmed milk represents the peak of human achievement to date. Any idiot has always been able to get ordinary cow milk, I say, but the leap up to skimmed milk requires a stroke of brilliance and sublime separation technology, which has only been made possible in modern times. And, in fact, I fear that humankind will progress no further. Skimmed milk will probably always reign supreme. But it does give us something to aspire to.

Skimmed milk ennobles mankind.

How many weeks is this supposed to go on for? he asks. As many as necessary, I say. Necessary for what? he asks. Time will tell, I say. And also I need some batteries and a few other small items from the shop. How much meat are we talking here? he asks. You can have what I've got in the sack here today, up front, and if this deal continues after Christmas, you'll get more. Done, he says, and gives me his hand.

This is great. It's a victory for the hunter-gatherer culture. Knife-slaughtered elk is exchanged for milk and other consumer goods. This is a breakthrough.

Maybe the world can still be saved.

Inside the shop I meet my wife of all people.

She's usually at work at this time of day, but obviously not today. She has her reasons, I suppose.

Hi there, I say.

You look dreadful, she says.

I'm not exaggerating when I say my wife thinks it's strange that I'm living up in the forest now. She doesn't think much of it, it seems. I don't blame her. I don't know that I think much of it myself. My father had just died and been buried and my mother and my sisters and I had sorted out all the practical details and I was out cycling. That was in the springtime. And it was a joy to cycle in the forest again after a long winter. Of course I cycle all year. To work and home again. I'm a cyclist. Maybe I am a cyclist first and foremost. No road conditions can hold me back. In winter I use studded tyres. I've got a helmet. Cycling gloves. Specially designed pants and jackets. A cycle computer. Lights. I cycle four thousand kilometres a year. And I think nothing of snapping off window screen wipers when cars don't behave. I bang on bonnets. I bang on side windows. I shout myself hoarse and I'm not frightened when motorists stop and want to have a go at me. I argue them into the ground, sticking to my rights as a cyclist. And I move around fast. Much faster than cars. Best of all is the morning rush hour. For example, down Sognsveien, across Adamstuen and on down Thereses gate and Pilestredet. There are loads of cars and often several trams. The trams stop in the middle of Thereses gate and as there's almost always oncoming traffic, the cars have to stop too, but I pull the bike up onto the pavement, steer well to the right of those about to get on the tram and shoot out again onto the road four to five metres in front of the tram and with plenty of time to spare before the tram sets off again. The pavement is a bit higher than normal just there and not only that there's a slight incline, it's a bit risky, and sometimes I land with both wheels wedged between the tramlines. It's showy, but I don't make a big song and dance about it. Whoever sees it, sees it. Perhaps some of them might be inspired to buy a bike. The thought of that is reward enough. I feed off that for the rest of the day while cycling to the next hurdle, which is the Bislet roundabout where I've also got a consummate technique that occupational drivers dislike and which may not be entirely legal. But as a cyclist you're forced to be an outlaw. You're forced to live on the wild side of society and at odds with established traffic conventions which are increasingly focussed on motorised traffic, even for healthy people. Cyclists are an oppressed breed, we are a silent minority, our hunting grounds are diminishing all the time and we're being forced into patterns of behaviour which aren't natural to us, we can't speak our own language, we're being forced underground. But be warned because this injustice is so obvious, and it cannot surprise anyone that anger and aggression are accumulating in cyclists and that one fine day, when non-cyclists have become so fat that they can hardly manoeuvre themselves in and out of their cars, we will strike back with all our might and main.

I am a cyclist. And I'm a husband and a father and a son and an employee. And a house owner. And lots of other things. We are so many things.

Well, I was out cycling. This spring. And then I fell. Quite badly. As you know, the path goes downhill into the forest. And the margins are often small. I had left a kind of path and found myself in the heather on my way down a gentle slope when the front wheel got stuck between two rocks. I flew over the handlebars and hit my hip on a root and the bike landed on my head as well. I was knocked flat. At first it hurt like hell. I couldn't move. I just lay still, looking up at some branches swaying in the breeze. And for the first time in several years everything was so quiet. Once the worst of the pains had subsided I experienced a blissful peace. There was only forest around me. The usual mixture of all types of complex feelings and thoughts and duties and plans was gone. Suddenly there was just forest. And I didn't have any of the enervating children's songs on my brain. Which I usually had. The songs that accompany the films my son and his chums watch on DVD. They're so insistent, so insidious. And they sit so heavily on my central nervous system. When I fell they'd been buzzing round my brain for months. They had been tormenting me for the whole winter. When I was at work, in my free time and when my father died. I considered seeking help because of it. Pingu, for example. This German-produced video-penguin that my son loves. Baa, baa, bababa, baa, baa, bababa, baba, baba, baba, baba, baba, baba, baaa, ba, ba, baa, BAAA! It could churn round my head for days on end. From when I opened my eyes in the morning until I went to sleep at night. When I was having a shower, having lunch, cycling to work, at meetings, cycling home again, shopping for tea, fetching the kid from the nursery school, and so on and so on. It was Pingu morning, noon and night. And on other days it was Bob the builder. For crying out loud. Booob the builder, can we fix it? Yes we can! Boom, boom, boomboomboomBOOOM! Or the Teletubbies. Horror of horrors. These, pardon my language, bloody quasi-cuddly figures which apparently were devised by a British psychologist to satisfy small children's curiosity and hidden needs. It grooves like crazy if you're two years old, but drives all the rest of us up the wall. Tinky Winky! Dipsy! La La! Po! Teletubbies. Teletubbies. Say HE-LLO! You feel like shoving them through a compost grinder. And Thomas the Tank Engine. Well, OK. Perhaps not so bad. At least not the first fifty to sixty times. With his optimistic Ta-ta-ta-ta-tata-taaaaaa, ta-ta-ta-taaa-ta, ta-ta-ta-taaaa-ta and so on, accompanied by punctiliously constructed model railway landscapes which look a bit like England even though in fact the stories take place on the island of Sodor where the tiny engine happily chugs hither and thither with its carriages Annie and Clarabel and its locomotive friends Percy and Toby and James and whatever they're called, as well as Harold the helicopter, Bertie the bus, Terence the tractor and the fat controller, or Mr Hat as we call him in our house, who constantly praises the trains when they've done something good, and that's quite often. My word, you're a useful little locomotive, Thomas, I can hear him say, or he can be tough like the time when the big locomotives got on their high horses and refused to pull their carriages themselves. He didn't want to know.

But Mr Hat was gone from my mind as I lay there in the heather. The songs had fallen quiet. And by some miracle all my bathroom thoughts had called it a day. I could hardly remember the last time I wasn't thinking about the bathroom. But now it had gone from my mind. All of a sudden I wasn't thinking about whether we should have Italian tiles or Spanish ones or matt or gloss, or whether we should simply

treat ourselves to glass mosaic, which of course my wife was really keen on. Not to mention colour. I wasn't even thinking about colours. Not about blue. Not about green. Not about white. It wasn't that I no longer cared about the colour of the ceiling or the tiles, but the very idea of it had simply disappeared. I had been spared this eternal merry-go-round in my head. And I wasn't thinking about the mixer taps, either, even though they are available in seven hundred different types and can be delivered in six weeks if they are in brushed steel or quicker if you're happy with the standard model, but why make do with the standard model, or the bathtub which we'd had to discuss the same day as USA and England had begun their campaign in Iraq. I remember being irritated when I discovered that now we would also have to take a stance on this war. It was very distracting. As if it wasn't enough to have to decide on all this bathroom stuff. Now we would have to take sides in Iraq. I didn't like things going on in the world which in effect reduced what I used my brainpower on to trivia. Not only did I not have my perspectives clarified, but I didn't want them to be. For weeks it had irritated me that they couldn't wait to start the bombing down there until we had finished doing up the bathroom. To hell with them, I thought. Should we go for the Polish tub which was considerably cheaper than the Swedish one which we were also quite fond of? Or should we take a hard line and consistently go for quality over economy? After all, there were good and bad things to be said about both tubs.

It wasn't as if the Swedish one was better in every respect. We discussed where to place the bath and drew up lists of the pros and cons of the Polish and Swedish models while the bombs rained down on the Euphrates, or maybe the Tigris, or both, on the TV, though we had turned down the sound, and this process is so exhausting, so absorbing that if you suddenly don't think it's important any more the whole project collapses, and perhaps the marriage, too.

And I wasn't thinking about the toilet, either, as I was lying in the heather. Whether it should be wall mounted, which is the most stylish at the moment, or whether we could make do with a more classical floor-mounted model. And the conversations with the plumber were also light miles away that afternoon in the forest. Especially the upsetting conversation when he expressed his opinion that the first plumber had made it impossible for the poo to get to where it should be going in the concrete and, for that reason, in a few seconds he was going to set about breaking up the whole floor and installing new pipes.

All that was gone. There were a lot of things I suddenly wasn't thinking about any more.

What on the other hand I *did* think about as I lay injured in the heather, letting the spring sun warm my face, was that my father was gone and would always be gone and that I had never really known him and that I didn't even feel anything special when my mother told me he was dead. He had died in the course of the night. Very suddenly. And very peacefully.

23

But in the heather all of this hit me with its gravity. The drama of it all. You're here and then you're not. From one day to the next. I saw it in a flash and realised that the difference is so overwhelming that the mind has to acknowledge its limitations and pass. All the things you can be and have, and then at the drop of a hat all things you cannot be and have because you have been and had for the last time. It's a repugnant construct. One of the alternatives contains everything and the other nothing. The emptiness following from these thoughts, combined with the bang on the head, caused me to drop off for a while. On waking I thought of something my sixteen-year-old daughter had said a few days earlier when we were sitting in a café after seeing *Lord of the Rings – The Two Towers* at the Colosseum cinema. She'd seen it eleven times before and now she considered that it was shameful that I hadn't seen it. Anyway, she no longer wanted to accept that her father couldn't be part of what for her was an adrenalin rush of historic dimensions. She had lain in a queue on the pavement for a couple of weeks to get tickets for the premiere. She and her boyfriend and her girlfriends and their boyfriends. Dressed as elves. We had had a few tough sessions with the school to get them to accept her being absent for so long in the middle of the school year, but she is a model pupil and the English teacher had vouched for her, and what's more Tolkien is great when it comes to stimulating young people's curiosity, they say, so, fine, and we've got a warm sleeping bag and all that. Anyway. In the film there is a sequence when the evil Saruman, incidentally very reminiscent of the late Hamas boss – the one with the white hair and beard who was in a wheelchair and said in a squeaky voice that the Palestinians would never give in no matter what – has his mines and tower dramatically destroyed after he had spent a long time rearing what are known as orcs, bad troll-like monsters whom he has now sent on a mission to kill everything good. His plans are thwarted by some living trees which the hobbits have persuaded to go into action. Among other things they destroy a dam with the result that the water floods out and causes a lot of damage to Saruman. On the way out of the cinema I happened to say that it would be quite some time before Saruman built a new tower at the foot of a dam. My daughter let the comment pass, but on arriving at the café she had a wild look in her eyes. I was keen to know what was up with her, though I wouldn't say that I was afraid of what she might come out with. From my perspective, she was so inscrutable that I was constantly on the alert for anything. Teenage girls have always seemed mysterious to me, not least when I was their age. Since then the distance between us hasjust increased, as is natural, and now of course I have myown, and the way I saw things that evening almost six months ago, the possibilities were endless. Take the most irrational thing you can think of and multiply it by the biggest number you can imagine, and you've got my daughter down to a T, I would say.

We arrived at the café and sat down. What's up? I said at

length.

She said she was shocked that my first comment after seeing an epic like that could be so cynical and so unaffected by the marvellous story I had just been immersed in.

Immersed? I'm not so sure about that, I said. We've seen an unusually expensive film about trolls. It was exciting. And I'm happy I've seen that side of life which means so much to you.

She said she couldn't accept that and it confirmed to her that the distance between her and me was as great as she feared, or if possible, even greater.

What do you want me to say? I asked.

We've seen a tale about good and evil, my daughter said. Do you feel nothing in your heart?

Yes, I certainly do. I've already said it was exciting. I understand that the ring is treacherous and that many people want to get hold of it, and it was very well done, he, what's his name, the transparent one who eats fish …?

Gollum, she said.

That's the one, I said. He was very well done. I don't quite know how they did it, but it was impressive. And the battle scenes were great and everything.

Do you know what your problem is, Dad? she said.

I shook my head.

You don't like people, she said. You're not a people person. And that's why I don't like you.

She got up and left.

She finished with me as if I were her boyfriend. That was actually quite impressive. For a moment I was almost proud of her. There goes my daughter, I thought, as she departed. She'll make out fine. Afterwards I ordered a beer and filed the event in the folder for irrational behaviour, thinking that in a couple of days she would be herself again. And indeed she was, more or less.

But lying there in the heather a few days later feeling the pain in my hip and the sun on my face I realised that my daughter was right.

I don't like people.

I don't like what they do. I don't like what they are. I don't like what they say.

My daughter had put her finger on my affliction. She had put words to something I had been trying to avoid coming to terms with for a long time. In recent years I had gradually distanced myself more and more from the people around me. I had lost interest in my work and also to some extent in my home. My wife had commented on this several times. She thought there was something wrong with her and I let her believe that for want of a better explanation. Admitting that it's you there's something wrong with is totally untenable. At any rate, as long as there's someone else ready to take the blame. I found myself almost constantly in a state where I registered what was going on in the world, but it never crossed my mind that it might have anything to do with me. And my daughter, in her elf outfit, said it did and hit the nail on the head.

I lay in the heather for a long time that afternoon. I threw up a couple of times and when after a while I got hungry I tried to knock down a squirrel with my cycle pump, but I failed. And then my wife rang wondering what had happened to me. I've fallen off my bike, I said, and tried to get to my feet. I managed somehow. I'm coming now, I said, and began to limp homewards supporting myself on my bike.

I had extensive grazing and a bruise which was yellow and reddish and the size of a wienerschnitzel, or something like that, and what I presumed was some kind of concussion. My wife bandaged the wounds and I said it wasn't her there was something wrong with, it was me. Oh yes, she said. What's wrong then? It's a bit too early to say, I said. But I was thinking a bit when I was lying in the forest. Good, she said.

The following days I didn't go to work. I got a sick note from the doctor and was told to take it easy for a week or two.

My daughter continued to watch *Lord of The Rings* again and again, and she made it clear she didn't want any more sarcastic comments from me, and my son, Gregus, God knows why I ever agreed to him being called that, watched his excruciating videos at all hours of the day and night when he wasn't in the nursery school. God bless the nursery school.

One day when my sick note was drawing to a close I began to flick through a pile of papers and pictures my mother had given me after my father had died. There were receipts and notes and lots of pictures of toilets, of all things. I rang my mother who explained that dad had been in the habit of taking pictures of toilets he had used in the final years of his life. He had never explained why he had taken the snaps and kept shtum. The result was hundreds of photos of toilets and trees and rocks and other places where you might have a piss outdoors. It struck me that I knew him even less well than I thought, but I liked the pictures and the thought of him having taken photos of all the places he'd had a piss. It was just like him. My father, the toilet photographer. As a consequence of this, or as a consequence of the feeling all this created in me, or at least hopefully as a consequence of something or other which had to do with something, I packed my bag on what seemed to be a sudden impulse, and which still feels like that, and wandered into the forest. I left a note on the kitchen worktop in which I briefly explained that I had gone for a walk in the forest and didn't know how long I would be gone but they shouldn't expect me for dinner. That's about six months ago now and I've only seen my wife a handful of times since then. She's been up to the tent twice to have sex and to persuade me to go home, and even though I've promised her both times to do so, I haven't. I say I'll go but I don't. I suppose, in a way, it's close to a lie, but so what, it's my life and I need to be in the forest for a while.

My wife is concerned by what people think and believe, as she says. It doesn't bother me any more. Nothing could bother me less than what people think. People can think what they like. In general I don't like them anyway and seldom respect their opinions. I haven't had any interest in our so-called friends for a long time. They pop by to see us and we them. It's an eternal hassle with dinners and kids and weekend walking trips and rented houses in the summer. And of course I've always strung along and as a result in a despicable way been part and parcel of it. That must have made them think when I headed for the woods. Doppler, of all people, they must have thought. A good job, a nice family and a big house in the process of being tastefully redecorated; and what should I say to those who ask? my wife has said several times with desperation in her voice. Say what you want, I said. Say that I've become manically obsessed with flora and fauna, say that I've gone mad. Say what you want.

I realise that my behaviour has been very trying for my wife and I've tried to explain that my little adventure has nothing to do with her. That's difficult for her to believe, I've noticed. At the start she suspected I had something going with another woman, but she doesn't think so any longer. Now, in a sense, she has resigned herself to the fact that I live in a tent even though she doesn't understand why. In good times and bad, they said when we got married. The problem with this is, of course, that any one time can be good for one person and bad for the other.

I'm pregnant, she then said, as we stood in front of the packet soup shelf in Norway's biggest ICA supermarket.

Crikey, I said. Again? We've barely had any sex since I moved out into the tent. As I said, it could only be a matter of two or three times. She came to see me at night and left again after a short session during which she could hardly be bothered to remove her outer clothing.

Due in May, she said. And if you're not back home by then you can forget the whole thing. Then it's over. Got it?

I hear what you're saying, I said.

And I'm sick of being on my own with the kids and not having your income any more, she said.

I understand that, too, I said. But I don't live in the forest for fun. I live in the forest because I have to be in the forest and you don't have the wherewithal to understand that because you've never felt that you have to be in the forest. And you always function so well and I function so badly, and you like mixing with people and it's easy for you, but I don't like to do that and it's difficult for me.

You're getting to be just like your father, she said, turning on her heel.

May was the last word I heard her say. And she stopped and repeated it. May.

This was a lot to digest in one go. Mixing with people down below was asking for trouble. I said that to the elk, but I didn't take sufficient heed myself. I should, of course, have made sure that my wife wasn't in the shop before I started swaggering around like an ordinary man. But now the

31

damage was done and sensitive information has changed hands and I'm going to be a father again. Horror of horrors. That means even more years with cynically composed children's songs from morning till night and I'm not sure my mental state is up to it. I wish I had a smaller penis. A penis my wife didn't yearn for. A teeny weeny limp organ she could live without. But you have to live with the organ you've been allocated and I've never ever seen an advert or an email offering a reduction in the size of such organs, and one saving grace of children is that, despite everything, they provide a bit of charm which, in small doses, can be something special. But birth and death. It's a revolting circus. My father disappears and a new life appears. One I never knew is replaced by another which I will never ever really know.

And if there's one thing I am not becoming, it's like my father. How could she say that? I hate it when she blurts out things like that. As if she knows things I don't. As if she's been thinking about it for a long time and suddenly decides to share a bit of her knowledge with me, but only a bit, the tip of the iceberg, only a hint, so that I have something to chew on, so that I can work out the rest of the picture myself. This is a technique she often uses and next time I see her I'm going to tell her to stick it up her arse.

I'll call the calf Bongo after my father, I decide as I'm strolling back into the forest. Even though my father wasn't called Bongo I'll name the calf Bongo after him. Sometimes you've got to be open to associations of this kind.

And in the sack I have some milk, some flour, some eggs, some oil and other staples, but above all milk, of course, as well as animal lotto which I exchanged for some meat in the book shop. Almost half a kilo it cost me. The elk is versatile and can be used in multiple ways. And, talking of milk, I stop on the edge of the forest, bid farewell to the last houses and knock back a litre. I carefully fold up the carton and take it along to start the fire.

In fact, I only live a hundred metres inside the forest, but nobody ever comes past. People stick to the paths. And they're all over the place here. Hundreds of them. I live only a little way into the forest, but it's still deep forest because nobody ever comes by. Løvenskiold, the owner of the forest, knows nothing about it. For three days you are allowed to erect a tent in the same place, whereas mine has been here for almost two hundred. I don't think he'd like that, Løvenskiold wouldn't. And the right-wing voters who promenade on Sundays in their breeches or else when they have a few days off or are walking their dogs, they don't know anything, either. They rush past absorbed in their right-wing thoughts, no more than fifty metres away the whole time, on the way to Vetakollen to look out over the town and to receive confirmation that they live in one of the best places in town, and they have no idea that I'm there. While thinking whether they should invest another handful of money in low risk stocks or whether they shouldn't force their neighbour to

33

prune the tree which before very long will be blocking a little bit of their view over the fjord or some of the sun from their garden. I'm sitting in my tent and I don't like them, and they don't know and I like that. That gives me something. Strangely enough. I think it's all to do with how good it is to hide. That wonderful old-time pleasure of not being seen. Being as quiet as a mouse and crouching down and feeling confident that no one will find you. It's invigorating.

Bongo is almost beside himself with joy when I come back and we spend the rest of the day in the tent. We play board games and have a nice time together and I feel some of the old pally feeling I had at school. You just hang out together. Don't talk about anything special. But Bongo's hopeless at lotto. He's really going to have to pull himself together if he wants me to keep on playing. I particularly chose animal lotto so as to give him a fair chance, but while I cover board after board with foxes and beavers and squirrels and wood pigeons, Bongo doesn't match a single pair. He's quite incapable of remembering where cards are. I point them out to him and expect him to give me a little sign such as a sound or a nod or something, but nothing. Not a sound. Not a nod. Bongo, Bongo, Bongo, I say. You may not be the sharpest knife in the drawer. But you are a real friend. And a lovely pillow.

I've earned my last krone, that's for sure, I tell Bongo, as I lie enjoying my victory. He takes the defeat with great composure. I'll give him that. No airs or graces about him in that

34

department. But I've gone from being more interested in money than anything else to being as uninterested as it's possible to be in our culture. Throughout my studies I thought about money and profit and regarded those who studied non-finance subjects as complete prats, I say to Bongo. And now I discover that nothing concerns me less than not having money. It's completely insignificant. Like a Donald Duck joke. A bang on the head made all the difference. I was obsessed with money and organised my time and spent all my time and energy trying to accumulate as much of it as possible. Then I fall off my bike and get a bit of a knock on my head and hey presto, I'm not interested in money any more. Not in much else either, I have to admit, sadly, but I have some hope I soon will be. And maybe I also have the perquisites. I have a tent in the forest; I have loads of time and meat. And I've got Bongo, my new pal. It feels as if we've known each other for ever. And my wife is completely deluded if she thinks I'm going to go down to her and the new baby and the other people in May. I have no plans to do so. On the contrary, I have plans not to do so, I can feel. She'll have to come and fetch me. Carry me. And she won't be able to do that when she's in the latter months. No chance.

I've toed the line for so long.

I've been so nice.

I've been so bloody nice.

I was nice in the nursery school. I was nice in primary

school. I was nice in secondary school. At grammar school I was revoltingly nice, not only work-wise but also socially. I was nice without being a swot, without just fulfilling the requirements, I was sometimes rebellious and cheeky and was close to overstepping the mark with my teachers, and still they liked me more than the others, and to be able to do that you have to be nice in an almost infinitely disgusting manner, I can see that now. I was a nice student and had a super-nice girlfriend whom I married in a nice way with nice friends after being offered a nice job that gave the finger to other nice jobs. Later we had children to whom we were nice and we acquired a house which we decorated to look nice. I had been wading up to my neck in all this niceness for years. I woke up to it, went to sleep in it. I breathed niceness and slowly it was killing me. That's how it was, I tell myself. God forbid that my children should become nice like me.

But my daughter has been showing worrying signs of niceness and I think it was the right time to move into the forest, it was also good for her. My time in the forest, which she regards as bordering on madness, may make her unsure of herself and thereby help her to mark out a way which is less nice and make her achieve less and generally speaking lower the bar. Unless it's already too late. Unless this niceness has already taken root within her and has taken complete control. I fear this is the case because niceness is habit-forming. Once you've become nice there are no limits to what you will do to continue to evince positive feedback from the world around you. It's a self-reinforcing spiral that never needs to stop. You can be nice as a pupil and student and later you can be nice in your professional life, in your community life, you can be a nice partner and friend and spouse, a nice parent and consumer, in fact there is nothing you can't do in a nicer way than other people, you can be nice about getting old, you can get ill nicely, and you can die in a nice way, which no doubt I would have done if I hadn't fallen off my bike and hit my head. But now it's not going to happen. I'm going to die un-nicely and I'm never going to try to achieve anything again as long as I live. I'm not going to achieve anything. I have achieved for the last time and I have been nice for the last time.

Fortunately my son has not yet been infected with this niceness and I have some hope that he can still be saved. My absence may save him, I constantly think. Missing me may create some unease in him, a longing, an imbalance, I imagine, and this imbalance may save him from niceness. My wife could also do with being less nice. With me being away for such a long time she'll become exhausted and may start making mistakes. Probably she'll get tired and angry and unreasonable with the children, and she'll sleep less and hopefully lack the usual energy which makes her nice and dependable at work and unerringly leads to her having a bad conscience and there is little that makes her so un-nice as a bad conscience. I'm going to save the whole family by staying in the forest. They think it's a handicap living out here, but in truth it's the salvation for us all. We'll have a lot to thank the forest for, my family and I, should I decide to return one day.

However, I can't see anything that might make me leave. Up here I'm not at the mercy of other people, and other people are not at the mercy of me. Other people are protected from my sarcasm and spitefulness, and I am protected from their niceness and stupidity. To me, it's a great arrangement.

Moreover, I'm getting used to solitude. I'm learning to live with it. As my father did. Perhaps without knowing. He was completely alone, my father. He had my mother for a great part of his life, but was alone all the same. In the last forty years of his life he had me and my siblings, but was no less alone for that. What was in his mind when he awoke in the morning, when he went to bed or when he went skiing or photographing toilets, I have no idea. Never did have. It's all gone now. And you can argue that it never existed because it only existed in him. Maybe there was something there and maybe not. It's like with Schrödinger's cat. You put a cat in a box with an atom of some radio-active material which, as it breaks down, triggers a mechanism which releases a fatal acid. But as you can't see inside the box you won't know whether it's happened or not. And therefore you have to accept that the cat is both alive and dead. My father lived in a box like that. Maybe he thought a lot and maybe a little. Maybe he felt okay and maybe not. He was both fully alive and completely dead at the same time. And now he's just dead.

We're born alone and we die alone. It's just a question of getting used to both of them. Being alone is fundamental to the whole construct. It is, so to speak, the corner stone. You can live with other people, but *with* generally means *next to*. And that's fine. You live side by side with others and for short, happy spells you can perhaps even live with them. You sit in the same car, eat the same dinner and celebrate the same Christmas. But that's not the same as being in the car together, eating dinner together or celebrating Christmas together. It's two extremes. Two planets. And now, by the way, they've found a heavenly body some say is a new planet and some say isn't. We believe we know so much, but in reality we don't even know what planets are, and even less who our fathers are. Or were. And you certainly don't know, I say to Bongo. You have no idea who your father is. Perhaps he lives in a box, too. In a box in the forest. The only thing you know for sure is that he's an elk, I say. And most probably quite a big elk, since he managed to mate with your mother, who herself was quite a size, not to say large. You're going to be big too, I say, and take him outside the tent and measure him against a fir tree. I see to it he keeps his head up, and place a book on top and cut a notch in the tree and carve in the date. So that we can keep track of how quickly you grow, I say.

A few days later, in the evening, as the fire is burning out, it occurs to me that the comparison between Schrödinger's cat and my father was too nice. I was trying to be nice again.

Even when I'm alone and I've decided not to be nice, I'm nice. It's a sickness.

Another, and in many ways, rather disturbing piece of information my mother gave me about my father was that during one of their many journeys to southern Europe, after an evening of good food and drink, if I understood her correctly, he had said that if he died before her she should make sure he was buried with a rhythm egg shaker. She was to put it in one of his suit pockets, he had said, and then she should tell the undertakers to dress him in the suit. She had taken him seriously even though the context had been Mediterranean and animated. And that was as much as my mother could remember; the only time in his life my father had used the expression 'rhythm egg shaker'. After he died we had a lively discussion about whether we should comply with his wish or not. My sister didn't think we should, but in the end we did. I went to a music shop and bought a red egg shaker. It wasn't very expensive and I shook it a few times as I left the shop to see if it worked. It was impressive. Exciting, in a way. And I had no problem imagining how it could helped to build up a hypnotic atmosphere when combined with several other instruments. First of all, a base rhythm, of course. Afterwards a more complex beat with intriguing syncopation. And then the egg shaker on top. As a kind of sublime seasoning. You don't think about it when it's there, but you can feel there's something missing when it's not.

That's the way it is with the egg shaker. And at the same time that's how my father is. But, to my knowledge, he never expressed any particular liking for rhythms or rhythm instruments. Perhaps he had had a bit to drink that night on southern shores and was happy and his head was full of the Mediterranean music which would have accompanied them through the night, and with a sudden flash of insight, the kind one sometimes has, it struck him his life ought to contain more rhythms, more dance and music and abandon, and fewer of the normal, dutiful and tedious things, you can easily slip into this kind of thinking, in flashes, there's nothing wrong with that, virtually everyone does it, I assume, one's life is filled with something or other it shouldn't be filled with and we notice it lacks something that others have got, for instance rhythms or happiness or depth or children or something that is generally felt to be good and meaningful. My father may have had such a moment down there in southern climes. Or it may have been an attack of nerves about the hereafter and a notion that an egg shaker might somehow be able to assist him on his way, that he could conjure himself up with it after death, that it could accompany him and help him to tackle obstacles and challenges. I'm speculating, naturally. But I know he read a lot. And what he read, by and large he kept to himself. He read classical literature. And there's a lot of death in that, I have learnt, and not so little about various kingdoms of the dead and what you have to do to get there, and so on. But I'm sure there are very few egg shakers in classical literature. No egg shakers in ancient Greek literature, I'm guessing. And not a lot in Roman. So where my father got this idea from is nothing short of a mystery. But now they're both under the ground. Dad. And the egg. I hope they can work something out, given time.

Before going to sleep, both Bongo and I go for a piss in the usual place and look out over the town and the fjord. The night is cold and clear and I notice that there are lights in some of the windows at the Meteorological Institute. They must be busy day and night, I suppose. The weather has to be tracked and analysed and models have to be made. There's no end to it. The weather never finishes and never has a break. And the snow is long overdue. Last year it came early and stayed. It stayed from back in October, but this year there's not a snowflake in sight. Just sun and unmitigated glee for everyone. But I would rather have snow. Snow is the only weather I really like. Nothing makes me less grumpy than snow. I can sit by a window for hours watching it fall. The silence of snowfall. You can use that. It's best when there's background lighting, for example a street lamp. Or when you go outside and let it flutter down on you. That's real riches, that is. That's more fun than anything you can do yourself. And, what's more, I enjoy shovelling snow. Can't have enough of it. Furthermore, I like the fact that there are people who don't like snow. Who become irritable when the snow arrives.

Who, after a whole lifetime in Norway, haven't managed to accept snow and still allow themselves to be riled by it. So I gloat when it snows. There is an element of *schadenfreude* in it. But now the buggers at the Meteorological Institute are taking the snow away from me. The snow has become fickle and I'm not even sure it will ever come back, and that's hard to bear. I would have preferred snow to almost anything. To most people. Perhaps even to you, Bongo, I say as we shake off the last drips. But it's a hypothetical question, so let's not dwell on it, I say. Don't think too much about it. Yes, I like you too, Bongo. You're OK. But you're not exactly snow.

december

As a teenager I found it intolerable that so many people in Africa lived in poor conditions while I had it so good. I sat listening to *The Wall* and felt this on many an evening. Most things seemed depressing and unjust and I saw no end to them. But then this phase passed. As suddenly as it had come. And nowadays I hardly give it a thought. Nowadays I'm as hard up as most people in Africa, I suppose. I live from hand to mouth. I'm a hunter-gatherer. I spend just as much time fetching water as your average African. If I'm very thirsty I might dip my bottle in the marsh up here, but the water is brown and stagnant and must have been here for a thousand years, so I prefer to go to one of the streams in the area. But you can't rely on streams. At times they dwindle to nothing and I can't collect water in any practical way. Nowadays I'm the one who's in Africa, I muse. In a sense, I'm under-developed, apart from my organ which is more on the over-developed side, and while the world around me may consider that I need help, I'm proud, just like Africa, and I would prefer to cope on my own. The biggest difference between Africa and me, I suppose, is that I don't like people, whereas Africa likes them a lot. It's a characteristic trait of Africans that they like to be surrounded by people, by friends and family, whereas I shy away from people, from friends and family, that's a characteristic trait of mine. Beyond that, we're like two peas in a pod, Africa and I.

Well, I spend a lot of time fetching water. Not to mention milk. But the deal has worked. The ICA boss puts out the milk he said he would put out. And I take it. So the need for liquid is covered. And I get vitamins and minerals through the milk, and also from Bongo's mother, of whom I still have quite a lot left. But I can't satisfy the need for sweet things anywhere. I haven't tasted anything sweet since the berry season finished and that's over a month ago. That makes me a trifle uneasy. I am, after all, like every other person, a finely tuned piece of machinery that has to be lubricated in the right way to function properly. Too much of anything is wrong and too little is just as wrong. Without sugar, things go downhill for me, and I start getting edgy when I notice that I've been walking around the tent like a sick animal for hours, just thinking about sugar, and after a few days of this unease I take Bongo down with me to Düsseldorf's house. From experience I know that Düsseldorf keeps chocolate in the house. He's mad about chocolate, is old Düsseldorf. And I've taught Bongo to carry things. I've sewn two bags or panniers or whatever you call them from his mother's hide, and I sling them over him and tie them under his belly. It works a treat and Bongo doesn't seem to mind. He's happy as long as he can be with me. He's my pack elk. And he carries wood and water and milk as if he's never done anything else. We stand watching Düsseldorf's activities at our leisure from the perimeter of his garden. He's making another model kit. I can't see what it is, but he's fully concentrated and is working with tweezers and glue. He's been on his travels again. On the kitchen worktop there is the biggest Toblerone that money can buy. It weighs four and a half kilos; it's over a metre long and as wide as my thigh. I've often seen bars like that myself. At Kastrup and other airports I used to fly on business before moving into the forest. But I've only ever bought the small ones. I've never dared to go the whole hog and buy the big one. It was being nice that held me back, I recollect. Always being nice. Small Toblerone bars are nice. They demonstrate a father's consideration for his family. He remembered them. He thought of them. But big Toblerone bars are too big to be nice. They're extreme and say dark things about the buyer. He's got an eating problem. He's lonely. He's weird. He's capable of anything. I notice that I respect this side of Düsseldorf. This ability to think big. And this evening he's airing the house. The back door is ajar because he's airing the house and he's doing this because he's a smoker. Even smokers who live alone air their houses. That's the pretty pass that things have come to now. And I can take advantage of that. I tell Bongo to stay behind a bush, as quiet as a mouse, and I sneak over to the door and in I crawl, along the kitchen floor, to the Toblerone, to the enormous, not to say monstruous,

Toblerone that every gram of me desires, it's more than a desire, I have a craving for sugar, a physical urge for sugar, and with this chocolate I will be assured of a supply of sugar for months, maybe for a whole year, and I stretch out my arm over the worktop and pull the behemoth towards the edge, closer and closer to the edge, and soon it's on the edge and teeters, and I don't make a sound, as indeed hunter-gatherers never do, we've never made a sound while at work, we've been quiet for forty thousand years, and now I almost have it, and I stretch, stretch out, oblivious to Düsseldorf getting to his feet, coming into the kitchen, I'm in the concentrated mode that filters out unnecessary noise, and the mode defines Düsseldorf's arrival as unnecessary, it's a fatal misjudgement and I don't suspect a thing, I'm like a retard, then he suddenly rounds the corner to the kitchen, sees what is about to happen, runs over to the Toblerone and grabs it and there is a tussle. I refuse to let go of the huge chocolate bar and Düsseldorf holds on tight, it's man against man, a classic showdown, and even though on paper there's no doubt I'm stronger than he is, I see myself becoming a startled witness to Düsseldorf gradually wresting the Toblerone out of my hands and hitting me on the head with it several times, hard. I black out, and on coming to again, I'm lying trussed up like a chicken, as they say, unfortunately, on Düsseldorf's kitchen floor, which by the way has been laid with brown linoleum.

The hours pass and I can hear Düsseldorf's model-building

noises from the sitting room. He continues his activities undaunted and leaves me lying there. That testifies to an impressive introversion. He's a complete obsessive.

What are you making? I ask at length.

Model-building noises.

What are you making? I repeat.

I assume it was you who stole the jam and meat from the cellar, he says.

I'm afraid it was, I say. I did take a few bits and pieces at one time, but I've stopped now.

You stopped because I had an alarm fitted, Düsseldorf says.

You could be right about that, I say.

And now you've started again, he says.

I have a pressing need for sugar, I say. I must have sugar.

He resumes his model-building. Then I hear him put something on the table and get up.

He comes into the kitchen, unwraps the Toblerone and cuts off a chunk with a kitchen knife. He gives me the chunk.

Straight into my mouth.

Aha! my body thinks. Sugar! My insides are filled with silent cheering. They didn't require much. That's the way we're constructed. So bloody banal.

Düsseldorf goes back to the sitting room.

So you make models, do you? I venture again after a while.

Yes, I make models, Düsseldorf says.

I assume he's going to go on, so I lie there quietly waiting, but obviously he's said his piece.

What are you making? I ask again.

I can hear him putting something down on the table and then he goes quiet.

I sense a kind of annoyance. He carries on working.

I'm making a German Steyr Type 1500A/01, he says eventually from the sitting room.

I wait for him to say more, but there is silence again.

I see, I say.

The Germans were good in the first phase of the war, he says. And part of the reason for that was that they had good equipment. They had good vehicles, good tanks and aeroplanes and so on.

Silence again.

But as far as I remember they didn't do so well in the latter part of the war, I say, wriggling noiselessly towards the back door.

No, Düsseldorf says. They didn't. But things went well at first. And, as I said, they had good vehicles. The model I'm making was manufactured in Austria and was available in five different weight categories. This one weighed one and a half tons and was used a lot as a staff car, breakdown truck and ambulance.

A versatile machine then, I say.

That's right, says Düsseldorf. Four-wheel drive. Three point five litre V8 engine. Eighty-five horsepower.

Mhm, I say, just reaching the door when I realise that Düsseldorf has taken the precaution of tying my foot to the radiator under the worktop. With an effort I stick my nose out and signal to Bongo to come over. He's still as quiet as a mouse behind the same bush. He's the most obedient elk in living memory, and now he's crossing the lawn and coming to my rescue. I stick my hands out and Bongo starts chewing and gnawing at the rope binding my hands together.

There is nothing like man and animal working in close collaboration against the forces of evil.

Why are you making that particular one? I ask, straining my voice so as not to reveal a) the fact that I have moved across the room, b) that I'm sitting in an impossible position and c) that I'm not in the slightest bit interested in why he's making that particular model.

He doesn't answer.

Not that it's any business of mine, I say. I suppose you have your reasons.

Yes, says Düsseldorf. I do.

Bongo bites through the last fibre of the rope and my hands are free. I loosen the knot around my foot and get up. My first impulse is of course to make a dash for the door, never to darken it again, but I sense at once I'm in thrall to the Toblerone. Firstly because I fancy some chocolate for chocolate's sake and secondly because I want to show Düsseldorf who's boss when the chips are down. I tiptoe over and grab the monster Toblerone. You're mine, I say to myself.

And I've bloody deserved you. Standing there with the grotesquely large bar under my arm, I suddenly feel I'm in charge and would like to steal a very quick glance round the corner into the sitting room to see with my own eyes how sad it is when an ageing man does something as pathetic as making a model of a German Steyr Type 1500A/01. Anyway, I've never seen the sitting room before. I've always come in through the back door, gone down to the cellar and out again.

I move towards the corner, without a sound, in the usual hunter-gatherer fashion, but this time with all channels open, one sound from the sitting room now and I'll be gone before Düsseldorf knows what's going on. I peep in and see Düsseldorf's concentrated back bent over a large table overflowing with model paraphernalia. I allow my gaze to drift further into the room and the sight that meets my eyes is amazing, indeed it borders on the shocking. Düsseldorf's sitting room is a battlefield. Quite literally. A battle is being fought in his room. Over perhaps 50 to 60 square metres. My knowledge of war is not extensive, yet I can say with more certainty than guesswork that this battlefield is from the Second World War. The colours and the whole iconography of this tableau in Düsseldorf's sitting room match my conceptions of the Second World War. With a richness of intricate detail approaching reality and thus also joyous insanity, Düsseldorf has built a landscape in the biggest room of his house. It represents a small town with the outlying district. I can see a built-up area, private houses, railway lines, open fields and a couple of farms on the other side of a river or canal furthest away by the large sitting room window. And there are trees, street lamps, fire hydrants. All the visible infrastructure that a real town in the world has, this unreal town in Düsseldorf's sitting room also has. It has to be a copy of a real town, I imagine. As it was at some point or other during the Second World War. The town is heaving with soldiers. They stand behind house corners, railway carriages and transport of all kinds and much more, shooting at each other. And it's winter. There's snow everywhere. Model snow. But it's realistic enough. The vehicles have left tracks in the snow. There are dead and wounded lying everywhere. It's a piece of war frozen in time. And I know in my bones that all the details are sure to match the reality that once must have befallen the outskirts of this town. The way the tanks, the supply lorries, the soldiers and everything else have been painted tell me that. The vehicles are the worse for wear, marked by the long, drawn out war. The soldiers are weary. Those operating the machine guns are doing their job in an efficient though disillusioned way while smoking apathetically. The houses are shell-pocked. Chunks of plaster have fallen off and lie in small heaps alongside the walls. Burnt-out cars are overturned and function as shelter for groups of soldiers reloading their guns or sitting and taking a breather. A locomotive pulling a huge cannon has derailed and some men are trying to lift it back with a crane. I estimate that there are a hundred vehicles here and probably three or four times as many soldiers. It must have taken years to make this, I reflect. Düsseldorf has spent years of his life recreating this Second World War winter scene and I think to myself: Respect.

Excuse me, I say quietly after observing this scene for several minutes. What is this?

Düsseldorf turns to me. He looks at me and the Toblerone stupidly protruding from under my arm, and then he surveys the war landscape.

The Ardennes Offensive, he says. December 1944. Christmas Eve that year, to be more precise. The town's called Bastogne. My father died there that day. He was shot driving a car like this. Düsseldorf holds up the car he is making. He was hit by a bullet in the left temple while delivering a battle update to General Manteuffel. It was twenty past two in the afternoon. It had snowed in the morning and is said to have started again an hour later. When the Offensive was over no one believed any longer that the Germans could hang on. The outcome of the war was as good as settled.

Düsseldorf turns his attention to the car and paints some tiny detail.

I survey the scene again. The clock faces on the church tower and the railway station actually show that the time will soon be twenty past two in this tableau, or scene, or whatever you call it. Düsseldorf is recreating his father's death. It's going to happen and it has happened and I notice that this fact makes an impression on me. He's reconstructing an event that is imminent and yet also happened many decades ago.

I'm sorry to hear that, I say.

It's OK, Düsseldorf says. It's a long time ago. I never met him. It's all about a moment in time. I've spoken to friends of his who survived. They said it happened at twenty past two. What sort of time is that to die? What sort of bloody time is that?

Perhaps it doesn't matter, I venture.

I think you're mistaken, Düsseldorf says.

OK, I say.

Düsseldorf keeps painting and I feel that the time to head for the woods is fast approaching, but instead of leaving I surprise myself by saying that my father is dead, too.

My father's dead, too, by the way, I say. He died this spring.

I'm sad to hear that, Düsseldorf says. Was he a good man?

I don't know, I say. I didn't know him that well. But he photographed toilets in the last years he was alive. I don't know if that's good or not.

I think it sounds good, Düsseldorf says. You shouldn't have let him die.

No, I say. I shouldn't.

I've been given some sherry and I'm sitting on the opposite side of Düsseldorf's model-making table watching him paint. With a pair of tweezers he's holding the minute piece of plastic which will become part of the rear axle and he is painting it a pale green colour with a small brush. He tells me his father was stationed in Norway during the first part of the war. Here in Oslo. He met Düsseldorf's mother and danced with her a couple of times and went for clandestine walks in the forest and got her pregnant. Afterwards he was ordered home and in late autumn 1944 sent to Belgium. He was supposed to have been a good officer and the Germans needed their best men for the Ardennes Offensive. It was seen as the last chance to halt the unfortunate downturn in fortune. He had originally come from Düsseldorf, and after Norwegian authorities had taken a softer legal line on names a few years ago Düsseldorf decided to take the town as his name. He's proud to be the son of a German soldier, he says. Not because the Nazis had fought for a good cause, but simply because things are as they are. My father was a German soldier, he says. And there's nothing you can do about it. But I have no reason to believe he was worse than any other soldier. On the contrary, I have some reason to believe he was a normal young man who along with millions of other normal young men had to take the consequences of being born into a given period of history. And since I never met him, I'll honour him. I'm building this scene to honour him. It's taken me six years. I've been doing it since my wife died. I started the day she was buried. I couldn't talk to her about my father. She didn't want to hear about him. I always had to pretend nothing had happened. And my mother never mentioned him, either. In a way I understand it, of course.

There are more appealing things to talk about than the fact that you were impregnated by a German soldier occupying your country. It wasn't until my mother died that I found some letters from my father, and moreover one from one of his subordinates saying that he was dead, and how it had happened. So when my mother and my wife died I could do as I wanted, and what I want to do is honour my father. And soon I'll have achieved my aim. I've often thought that when this officers' car is finished and I've made and painted my father I'll put them on the correct spot in my model and then shoot myself through the head. Sometimes I think I'll do that here at home and sometimes I incline towards going to Bastogne and doing it on the actual spot where my father died. I do know where it is, you see.

Düsseldorf gets up, still holding the tweezers with the plastic component and the brush, goes over to the model and points to a place at a crossroads. This is the spot, he says. And this was where he wrote to tell my mother about it. He points to a private soldier kneeling behind a battered wall. His name was Reiner. Decent man. He made model aeroplanes. I met him a couple of times before he died three or four years ago.

Düsseldorf sits down and continues to paint.

But something puts me off the whole idea, he says after a while. It's sentimental and unoriginal. So I don't know. I'll have to see. And what about you? he asks.

I'm alright thanks, I say. Things are going well. I live in the forest with an elk. Not far from here. I've got a tent.

 59

He looks at me.

May I ask why you live in the forest? he asks.

I don't like people, I say.

He nods.

Nothing you can say to that, he answers, putting down the brush and proffering me his hand.

Düsseldorf, he says.

Doppler, I say.

The day before the football international against Spain my wife comes to my tent and says she needs a break and that she has booked a long weekend in Rome with a girlfriend.

Rome, yes, I say, thinking in quick succession of the Pantheon, the Colosseum and the cardinals screwing around while wondering whether women have souls or not, and of Nero, of course, who killed his closest family and let the city burn. I don't reckon he liked people, either.

Rome in December, I say. Isn't it too cold?

No, says my wife.

OK, I say. Good idea. But what about the kids? Who'll take care of them?

You will, she says. And there's a parents' evening for Nora's class on Thursday and Gregus has to take fruit to the nursery school on Friday.

Fruit, I say. Where am I supposed to get fruit from? That's no good. I've got a tent to look after. And a small elk, on top of that.

Don't view this as a request, my wife says. These are instructions. It's something you have to do whether it suits you or not.

It goes without saying that our daughter is called Nora. My wife is partial to Ibsen, well, to theatre in general; she has no critical faculties, she watches anything and thinks it's all good. She thinks theatre productions are good because they're theatre productions and theatre is essentially good and our daughter had to be called Nora because Nora represents some of the earliest women's liberation we know. As far as I'm concerned, she might just as well have been called Master Builder Solness. But I didn't say that at the time. I was too nice. We both thought Nora was perfect even though my wife probably considered it more perfect than I did.

And now you're Nora, I say, it rolled off my tongue.

I beg your pardon, says my wife.

You're leaving your husband and children, I say. You're Nora.

No, *you* are Nora, my wife says. You left everything six months ago.

I am not Nora, I say. I'm Africa.

You need help, says my wife.

How are you getting on otherwise? I essay. Are you eating enough? Are you in good shape?

You need help, she repeats.

61

After my wife had left, Bongo had a long bout of the sulks. My interpretation is that he's jealous. He sees my wife as a rival, which as such corresponds with reality. But a wife is quite different from a pal, I explain. I'm married to her and have to act accordingly and of course I love her, too. But you and I are friends and we will always be friends and I can say loads of things to you that I could never say to her. Don't worry, I say, stroking his underbelly.

You and me, kiddo, I say.

I can hear the noise from the match against Spain down at Ullevaal Stadium. Curiosity drives me further up the mountain to try and look down on the game with binoculars, but all I can see is a corner of the pitch and bits of one goal. I see a ball go in and conclude from the roar that it hasn't exactly gone in Norway's favour. Later I hear the same sound two times more and infer that the game is over. Norway is not going to the European championship in Portugal. Fair enough. We didn't have any business going there anyway, or what do you think, Bongo? I say. And it's not easy to know what Bongo thinks, it really isn't, he keeps his cards close to his chest and doesn't reveal his real thoughts about Norway's manager, Semb. You can say whether you like him or not, can't you? I say. But he's silent. You can say whether he's a charismatic charmer, can't you, or whether he should go to hell? I say. Zero response. Then I choose to believe you think he should go to hell, I say. Correct me if I'm wrong. But he doesn't correct me and I'm not wrong. It's a bit of a shock, I say. You seem so friendly and soft and kind, but inside you're carrying around a lot of aggression. You'll have to work on that, I say. We've all got things to work on. I have my own crosses to bear. But I am a bit surprised that you go around wishing Semb ill. It's not hard to understand why you don't particularly like him, but to send him to hell? OK, well, why not? I suppose you know best.

I collect my son from the nursery school at the latest possible moment. I've been shying away from it the whole day. What should I say to him? How should I explain that for the last six months I've been living only three or four kilometres away, but have never got into contact? I've prioritised the forest. I've chosen to be in the forest with the silence and the elk rather than at home with him and his sister and Mummy. I've chosen the forest over work and things like trips to Smart Club to buy pallets of toilet rolls and magnum bottles of Lactacyd so that the whole family's nether regions can bear scrutiny at all times, and everything from Lego at half price to windscreen wash to high pressure washer and hot dogs on the way out. Gregus loves Smart Club. But now my member's card has probably expired, and I've chosen to live in the woods so I'll have to explain that when I meet him again in a while. I chose the forest over Smart Club and all the other absurd places you have to go when you have a family and live in the capital of Norway. This is obviously impossible for a three-year-old to understand, or maybe he's four, crikey, I think he's four. Time flies when you live in a forest. But he won't understand. The boy who sometimes wakes up in the middle of the night and asks if we can go to Smart Club won't understand anything and, standing by the nursery gate I know inside that I will have a problem explaining.

All the other children have been collected and Gregus begins to cry when he sees me. The nursery person doesn't recognise me and I don't recognise her. She asks me to prove my identity, which I can't do because I no longer carry around any ID, but I'm good old Doppler, I say, and I can tell her anecdotes about last year's Christmas party at the nursery if she wants, I say, while Gregus continues to howl and in the end I pull out my knife to cut off my beard, but the nursery person stops me and calls my wife who, I understand from the conversation, is on her way to the Pantheon by bus and as she passes through ancient Roman streets she confirms that I have a beard and otherwise look unkempt and wild.

Gregus calms down and we amble home with me trying to ask him normal questions about the manifold activities of a nursery day. He, for his part, wants to know why I look so weird. I say, as is the truth, that I'm living in a tent in the forest at the moment and that I've let my beard grow because it is simply easier to let it grow than to keep preventing it from growing. I also say that he will have a beard himself in a few years' time, but he dismisses that as nonsense.

At home we meet Nora who also reacts with shock at my

appearance. I say that I've been thinking of taking Gregus with me to the tent and letting him stay with me until his mother returns from Rome. Of course, she is also welcome to join us, I say, knowing very well that that is probably the last thing in the world she feels like doing. And she rejects my offer, as I thought she would. She's on the home straight of a project about Tolkien, she says, and would like to spend the weekend applying the finishing touches. It irks me to see how nice and conscientious she is and I try to urge her to have a party instead. Just imagine the wild party you could have, I say. All alone at home and so on. You could invite the whole school, I say. Let it all hang out. Let people smoke and run amok and dance and be happy. You need that kind of party when you're young. You need parties you can put in your locker and keep for the rest of your life, which define who you are. There'll be days when you look back on the wild parties you've had with more satisfaction than the good grades you got in your project, I say. But she doesn't believe me. You could have a little party, then, I say. My God, come on, girl. You've got the house to yourself. It's a heaven sent opportunity. And then you can come up to the tent afterwards and sleep off the booze and have some elk meat. She just sends me an old-fashioned look.

I hope you're not going to the parents' evening tonight, she says, but I say that's precisely what I'm going to do. Her mother told me to attend and attend I will. Is there anything in particular you'd like me to mention? I ask. Are you happy with the teachers? Are you being intellectually stimulated enough? Are you excused gym when you have your period?

She eyes me with disbelief.

'I would appreciate it if you didn't go to the meeting,' she says.

I go to the meeting. Partly because my wife told me to and partly because I don't want to hear later that Nora's parents don't care. The meeting has been disturbingly nicely organised. With the agenda written on the board and name cards on desks. I sit in Nora's seat by the window in the first row, and even though it's probably decades since there was any prestige in sitting in the front row I'm a bit depressed by that. I suspect Nora thinks it's great sitting here and being the best. The class teacher, a lady in her fifties, starts by saying that this class is one of the most resourceful she has ever come across in her time in education and she lists examples and tells us about a class trip to the Baltic which is due to take place soon. Although the class has been selling waffles for more than a year in the long breaks, they still need to put in three thousand kroner each, she says. It's a lot to ask, she knows, and it is voluntary after all, but they're going to both Tallin and Vilnius, two cities with quite a bit to recommend them, I'm given to understand. There is a wealth of history in the region, and a lot about the War and the Soviet Union, and a trip like this is a gold mine for such a strong class as this because it can be kept busy with it for ages afterwards. Reports can be written, wall charts and collages can be made, and furthermore contacts for life can be sealed.

Questions are asked concerning alcohol. I raise my hand and suggest that pupils be given permission to drink some alcohol, but the other parents do not agree. Come on, I say. Let the young ones have a free rein. Let them drink themselves silly and stagger home to the hotel as the cock crows. We're doing them a disservice by protecting them as we do, but I'm met by incomprehension. In fact, I have the impression that they consider me outrageous, not quite on this planet. Life has become like that. Cycle helmets and safety precautions everywhere. My daughter will have permission anyway, as much as she wants, I say in defiance, while the other parents look away.

Under Any Other Business I say that in my opinion the barter economy should be on the curriculum. Young people should be encouraged to exchange goods and services rather than buying everything in sight. The future of the earth depends on it, I say. For humans do not own the earth, I say. The earth owns us humans. Flowers are our sisters, and the horse, the great eagle, not to mention the elk, are our brothers. So how can you buy or sell anything? For who owns the heat in the air or the sound of the wind in the trees? And the sap in the branches contains the memory of those who have preceded us. And the gurgle of the brook carries within it my father's voice and in turn his father's. And we have to teach our children that the ground we walk on contains the ashes of our forefathers and that everything that happens to the earth will happen to us and that if we spit on the earth we are spitting on ourselves, and by the way, I say, while I'm at it, is anyone here willing to swap some fruit for elk meat? I take two to three kilos of meat out of my bag and smack it down on the desk. It's good meat, I say. Smoked, tasty. And all I want is a handful of bananas and some nursery-friendly fruit in exchange. No one takes me up on the offer until afterwards when we're on the way out. Then the father of one of Nora's nicest and poshest girlfriends comes up to me and says he would like the meat. And we go in his car to a petrol station where goes in and buys a carrier-bagful of assorted fruit and then drives me home. He comments that I look different and tentatively asks what I'm doing at the moment. I suppose he must have heard something or other from his nice daughter. I've moved into the forest, I tell him. I've handed in my notice at work and moved into the forest because it was the only sensible thing to do. He nods. The forest is fickle, he says, as I get out of the car, so be careful. You're wrong, I say. The forest is gentle and friendly. It's the sea which is fickle. And the mountains. But the forest is predictable and less confusing than almost every other place. Whereas you cannot trust the sea or the mountains or people in any way at all, I say, so you can place your life in the forest's hands without any qualms. For the forest listens and understands, I say. It doesn't destroy; it restores and allows things to grow. The forest appreciates and accommodates everything.

'OK, OK,' he says. 'You'll have to be careful nevertheless.'

'You should be careful yourself,' I say.

When I arrive home Nora has put Gregus to bed and is sitting watching TV. It's a documentary programme about how all those who worked on the *Lord of the Rings* films made friendships for life. They miss each other terribly now the filming is over, and some of them are down and lack the motivation to tackle new projects. Nora thinks it's sad, I can see. But she smiles to herself when the cast talk about wonderful, crazy things that were done and said in the make-up caravans and on the set. Life wasn't always a bed of roses however. Often they had to get up at the crack of dawn and sit for hours having the big hobbit feet put on. And Peter, the director that is, always had time for everyone and made them feel competent and important even though his head was full of the larger narrative and of the staging options necessary to communicate it in the best possible way to all Tolkien lovers around the globe. An extraordinary man, Peter. Big, teddy bear-like, fun to the tips of his toes and at the same time extremely competent and normal. I suppose I am not quite in his class. Film production is one of the last things I should try my hand at. I can imagine that you need crystal clear vision and energy to spend years of your life steering it past all the obstacles, and you have to motivate a huge number of people to do their best, although they may not have anywhere near the same conception of the totality as you. It's insanity, nothing less. The actors would hate me as much as I would hate them. I wouldn't be able to take the story seriously. Battle scenes between non-existent creatures. What is that? I would have created an apprehensive and spiteful atmosphere on the set, and the film would have become an apprehensive and spiteful film. No Oscars coming its way. And no nice, well-to-do teenagers queuing to secure tickets for the premiere.

It's a very good thing it wasn't me who made *Lord of the Rings* or any of the other films on release in the world. People are talented, it occurs to me. People get things done. And the world around me is going to continue being nice and talented whereas I've been nice and talented for the last time.

How was the parents' meeting? Nora asks at length.

It was fine. Hear you're going on a trip, I say. Exciting.

She nods, listening to Liv Tyler learning Elvish on TV. It was demanding, we're told. That's all I needed. Not only is it a dead language but it's a dead language that has never existed anywhere except in a diligent Englishman's imagination.

Elvish is a fantastically beautiful language, Nora says.

Doubtless, I say.

You can say so many things that you can't say in other languages, she says.

Such as? I ask.

For example, I love you, she says. It sounds pathetic in Norwegian and in fact it's beginning to sound pathetic in English, too, she opines.

But in Elvish it just sounds wonderful.

That may well be, I say. But how often do people of your age need to say they love someone? I ask.

You know nothing about that, Nora says.

I don't, I say. That's why I'm asking.

It's quite possible for someone to love another person even though they're young, she says, piqued.

And who is it possible for someone to love? I ask.

Boyfriends perhaps, Nora says.

Ha! I say.

Or Peter Jackson, she says.

I laugh my arse off.

Against my will I have to spend the night in the house. To tell the truth, the plan had been to carry Gregus up to the tent in my backpack while he slept but nice, conscientious Nora stopped me. Now they're both asleep and I have palpitations thinking about poor Bongo not knowing where I am. The little elk will be running around feeling all alone. He won't be able to go into the tent, either. After all, he hasn't got any hands. It's pretty limited what an elk can manipulate, from a fine-motor co-ordination point of view.

Apart from illicit visits to Düsseldorf's house and the odd trip to ICA it's six months since I have been in a building. My appetite isn't whetted at all. I walk around, restless. Fill my rucksack with the tools and dry foods I may need. Watch a spot of TV; there is the usual rich selection of tennis matches

 71

and reconstructed crimes and more or less fictional stories about the vicissitudes of human life. For me, watching TV is a compilation of all the reasons why I don't like people. TV is a concentrated form of everything that is repulsive about us. Those human qualities which in real life are already difficult to reconcile yourself with stick out like a sore thumb when they appear on TV. People seem like idiots. On TV even I would have looked like an idiot.

Everything which is human is alien to me.

Before my fall in the forest I spent my evenings at home with the family. I have always shunned organised leisure activities. So almost every evening was spent at home. We ate, watched children's TV, put Gregus to bed and then sat in front of the TV leafing through more or less interesting newspapers until the clock told us that it was time to pay bills on the Net. Always plenty of bills. Electricity, council tax, telephone, newspapers, plumber and nursery, as well as Nordberg Tennis Club which we regularly had deliver sixty-four toilet rolls straight to the door. We liked that. The old men up there keeping themselves busy with the organisation of the club. When they aren't maintaining or using the courts they drive around delivering toilet rolls to the neighbouring district. It's a kind of job for them. In that way they keep themselves alive and we have paper to wipe our bottoms with. But now I realise with a satanic grin that I have paid my last bill. I will never ever pay a bill again. Neither on the Net, nor in any other way. I will live from bartering or thieving or the forest. And when I'm gone the forest will live from me. That's the deal.

I sleep fully dressed on the sofa, but wake after a while to sounds at the veranda door. Someone is fiddling with the lock. Fascinated, I sit up on the sofa and study the technique. After a few minutes, and without any noise of note, a man comes into the sitting room. It takes some time for him to realise I'm there.

Good evening you there, I say.

He is startled, but gathers his wits.

OK, he says. You don't need to be frightened. I'm not violent. I'll be on my way right now. See, I'm going. He says moving towards the veranda door.

Just come in, I say, going into the kitchen and putting on the kettle.

Coffee? I shout.

Thank you very much, he says. But I don't know. Perhaps I ought to be moving on.

Join me now you're here, I say, stretching out my hand.

Name's Doppler, I say. Andreas Doppler.

I can see he thinks the situation is awkward, but in the end he proffers his hand.

Roger, he says.

Just Roger?

I'm a bit chary about giving my surname, he says, but folk

73

call me Toolman Roger. I used to work with scrap.

Interesting, I say.

You know what I'm doing here, don't you? he asks.

Yes, I say.

So you're not kind of backward? he asks.

No more than your average Joe, I say. Let's have a look at the tools you brought with you.

He holds out a bunch of various picklocks attached to quite a large key ring which in turn hangs from the end of an extendable ski lift card attachment, the type you often see in the Alps. This guy knows his way around, I think to myself.

Do you take anything in your coffee?

No thanks, he says.

I can't tempt you with something a bit stronger? I ask, hoping the flask of ethanol is still in the basement workshop.

Not when I'm working, says Toolman Roger.

Come on, I say. Drop your shoulders for heaven's sake. It's clean stuff.

He looks at his watch.

A little one then, he says

The alcohol is in its usual place and I pour us both one.

So you're out and about robbing? I say.

Yes, Roger says. I like this area. Lots of valuables and very few alarms. Higher up it's right-winger country with alarms everywhere, but down here folk vote left and think about the good in people, and they're rolling in it, too. For me that's an unbeatable combination. And you live here, do you? he asks.

Not at all, I say.

I see, he says. But you're spending the night here?

That's exactly what I'm doing, I say. I used to live here. And my wife and my children still live here.

Divorce, he says, nodding. Sorry to hear that. I know about all that.

No, I say. We're still married, but I've moved up into the forest. I live there in a tent with a little elk.

OK, he says, looking at his watch again.

I give him some more coffee and alcohol.

Tell me about your occupation, I say.

There's not much to say, he says.

I don't believe you, I say. You break into houses and steal people's things. You must be able to tell me something about it.

Well, he says, taking a swig. I try to do it in a decent way. I recce first and only enter where I know there's something worth having. I don't touch personal items. Never break anything. I know how unpleasant it is when burglars have been in people's houses and turned everything upside down. Of course I know some who do that, but I've always distanced myself from that kind of behaviour. By the way, is it alright if I smoke?

Smoke away, I say. My wife's in Rome.

I put the kettle on again, fetch an ashtray and pour another round.

I don't know that I should have any more, he says. I'm

75

driving.

You can take a taxi, I say. For once. Then you can pick up your car tomorrow. Underground to Ullevaal Stadium and over the footbridge. A doddle.

OK, Roger says. Go on then.

And the swag, I say. I suppose you spend it on drugs, do you?

Now you disappoint me, Roger says. You're tarring all burglars with the same brush. I don't touch illegal substances. I've got a family like you. But I don't have an unblemished record or education or anything else that might look convincing on a CV. Not only that, I've got a problem taking orders from others. There aren't many jobs I can get and the ones I can get I often don't want. But I try to steer clear of criminal elements. Which means there are not many opportunities left, apart from operating on your own. And I'm doing fine. I'm making ends meet. And by and large folk get their money back off the insurance.

It turns out that Roger is a great guy. He teaches me a bit about picking locks and gives me a handful of other tips about housebreaking. The more we talk and drink, the better I like him. The alcohol flows and we discover we have several mutual interests, especially as regards the open air life, forests and the countryside, and in the private confidences department Roger has been convinced for some time that he'll get prostate cancer like his father, he says, and he's not too keen on that, but recently he read that if you have 20–25 ejaculations a month that reduces the risk considerably. So he makes sure he has orgasms all over the place and he's found out that he particularly likes squirting his sperm on things that are not designed to be squirted on. It could be anything actually, he says, books, journals, crockery, anything at all, and the best thing about it is that his partner goes along with it. Roger squirts all over the flat and she's fine about it.

As day breaks I ask him what he had his eye on in this house.

You've got a Primare stereo set, he says.

True, I say.

Primare are good, he says. Swedish hi-fi at its best.

And you'd been thinking of nicking the lot? I ask.

I had, he says. The car's parked around the corner and I'd been thinking of transporting it in two or three trips.

Speakers as well?

Yes, he says. Audiovektor are good kit, too. Danish quality. There are a lot of Scandinavian hi-fi products in this area. That means money. You can just imagine what it costs to produce that kind of quality in our part of the world with our wage levels. It's obvious it's going to be expensive. But it has to be good. For you people it's not enough to listen to Bach or whatever the hell it is you listen to on equipment from Asia. That's just not good enough. You want that bit extra. And that costs thousands.

Which particular bit are you after? I ask.

 77

That would have to be the combined CD and DVD player, he says.

Take it, I say. In a way I've ruined your night. You've lost earnings because of me. So you can just take it.

No, he says. That's too much. I don't want to.

Yes, you do, I say. Just take it. My wife listens to the radio a lot, so I'm a bit reluctant to part with that, and the radio won't work without the amplifier of course, and it would be daft without the speakers, but you can have the CD/ DVD player. And I would appreciate it if you would take my son's DVD collection while you're at it. He has the full range including *Bob the Builder*, *Pingu*, the *Teletubbies*, *Thomas the Tank Engine* and more. I'll guarantee any modern child would be thrilled to have it. Have you got kids yourself?

I've got two, Roger says proudly and tells me their names and shows me photos he keeps in his wallet.

Good for you, I say, wondering where the box for the CD/ DVD player and the warranty are.

I give Roger instructions on how to find my tent and he promises to visit me up there, and when he leaves I stand on the terrace and wave to the taxi as it disappears from view.

Straight afterwards Gregus wakes up and comes downstairs to watch a film as he often does in the morning before going to nursery school.

Sorry, Gregus, I say. There's no film today. During the night a thief came and stole the DVD player and all your films.

Of course, he begins to cry and insists on us phoning the police. Without a moment's hesitation I grab the phone and pretend I'm making a dramatic call to the police and in the conversation let drop that they haven't caught him yet, but they have a full-scale search on. After putting down the phone I tell him I think this thief was quite a kind thief. A bit like the robbers in Cardamom Town. Basically good at heart. Let him keep the DVD player, I say. He needed it more than we did. And you can start saving up for a new one, I say. Anyway, you would soon have grown out of the films you had. Chin up. Look upon this as an opportunity, as a new beginning. As a Norwegian poet once said: It's the dream. Slipping into an unfamiliar bay in the early morning. That's what we're doing now, Gregus, I say. That's what we're doing today.

I deliver Gregus and the fruit to the nursery and then jog up to the forest to show Bongo I'm still alive. He's lying outside the tent, wet and cold, and I invoke higher powers and say it will never happen again, but Bongo is disappointed and fed up and remains aloof and dismissive until I have rubbed his fur for an hour in front of the fire and hummed snatches of old songs from our rich folk music heritage. Then we both fall asleep and when we awake it's already afternoon and we have to run to get to the nursery before it closes. I have neither the time nor the heart to tether Bongo at the edge of the forest, so he comes along. The nursery person rolls her eyes as I apologise for being late, but I quickly gather up Gregus's things and extricate myself from the situation without any further conflict and with some elegance, I think. This is Bongo, I say to Gregus after we have put a bit of distance between ourselves and the nursery. True, he's an elk, but nonetheless he's a good friend of mine and therefore of yours too, I explain. It doesn't take Gregus and Bongo long to get to know each other. Mentally they are the same age and they chase each other in and out of the trees as we head up the mountainside. When Gregus is tired he's allowed to sit on Bongo's back while I walk ahead holding Bongo by a rope. From a distance we probably look like a slice of bible history. Joseph, a strange donkey and a tiny, child-like Maria.

Gregus is a woodsman like his father. It's innate. The hunter-gatherer instincts are deeply rooted in his genes as they are in mine. We grill meat on a spit and relax, resting against Bongo's flanks, but as the hour of children's TV approaches I notice that his body begins to twitch. He hasn't got a watch and he can't tell the time anyway, but still the impulse is there, it's physical and tangible. He knows that there's something going on, but is unable to express it in words. I say nothing, and children's TV comes and goes without Gregus knowing what has come and gone. Gradually his unease passes and he runs off to play with Bongo outside the tent. He collects fir cones in the dark and I can hear from their conversation that he feels they're collecting cones together, even though Bongo is not able to collect anything at all. As bedtime approaches we play a round of animal lotto. Of course Bongo loses again, and for a moment I consider letting Gregus win, but it crosses my mind that victory can easily lead to the kind of one-upmanship all those nice people suffer from, so in the end it is me who wins and what's more I rub it in by making it quite clear that it was me who won and not him. Then he falls asleep in my sleeping bag beside the fire. I sit for a while and look at him in the light from the flames, thinking with pleasure that I definitely like him. I like my son and enjoy his company.

The next morning I hear sounds outside the tent. I take Bongo with me and go out and see a right-wing voter dressed in weekend breeches with a dog. He eyes the tent with annoyance.

You know you can't have a tent up for more than three nights in the same place, he says. I know, I say.

I suspect this tent has been up for much longer, he says.

Maybe, I say. And while we're at it I would prefer it if you didn't walk by here again.

You have no right to stop me, he says.

Of course not, I say. I'd just like to make the point that I would appreciate it if you took another route next time you went out walking.

We'll see about that, he says.

Who is it, Daddy? Gregus shouts from the tent.

Just a reactionary, I say. Go back to sleep.

81

I'm quite sure that I'll pass this way again, the man says. And I've made a note of today's date.

And what date is it? I ask.

The thirteenth of December, he says.

And spontaneously I begin to sing. Years of school parties have left such a deep mark inside me that as soon as the date is mentioned I begin to sing.

Night goes with silent steps, I sing quietly, Round house and cottage. Over the earth that the sun forgot, I continue as I am joined by Gregus's voice from the other side of the tent, Dark shadows linger, Then on our threshold stands, we sing with increasing passion, Whiteclad with candles in her hair, Saaaaantaalucia, Santa Lucia! We sing all the verses, and as the song fades away the reactionary says he's going to ring Løvenskiold if the tent's still here in two days' time.

Clearly the Christmas message of love doesn't have much effect on you, I say.

He doesn't answer.

And I suppose Løvenskiold is a friend of yours, I say.

Yes, fancy that, says the reactionary.

But who owns the air we breathe and the trees in the forest? I ask. Who owns the water in the stream and the song of the birds? Shouldn't I as a citizen of this country have a right to linger in the forest if I so wish?

Not in this forest, says the reactionary.

You're a true guardian of the status quo, I say, whereas I'm an enemy of the people. You want to conserve tradition while

I want to break it down. You want everything to stay as it is while I want it to change. You have a dog and I have an elk. You want to buy, I want to barter. There you have some of the differences between us in a nutshell, I say. And you can come here with your dog and kick up a stink, but you should know that I don't like your way of thinking, I don't like your clothes, I don't like your dog and least of all that self-satisfied smirk on your face. It's a smirk that only immense material security and prolonged right-wing voting can produce. And I not only don't like it, I can't stand it, and now you can clear off, I say.

He goes. But he turns a couple of times and makes it clear to me that this is not the last word and he's going to check if the tent is still here in a couple of days. Oooh, I'm so scared, I jeer in a childish voice. And it strikes me that six months ago a threat from such a smart reactionary type would have made me profoundly re-think whether in fact I was at fault, but now, in this new sylvan life of mine, it makes no difference to me, one way or the other. I feel unassailable. The reactionary and his crowd might constitute the cream of the legislative and executive power structure in this country, but he can't touch me. Because I have taken the step of moving into the forest and here other rules apply. Out here, it is not Oslo or Norway any more; it's the forest. And it's a separate country with separate little laws of logic, and the reactionary and his cronies can govern the rest of the country and sell each other cars and boats and properties and help each other with legal hair-splitting in rows with neighbours, they can shoot each other's elk quotas, award prizes to each other's dogs and employ each other's children as trainees and assistant directors after they've studied and travelled abroad, but out here in the forest they have no influence. The forest is not impressed by them. It treats them no differently from anyone else. Out here they can't touch me.

Why do you live in this tent? Gregus asks as we're eating breakfast by the fire.

Not quite sure, I say. But I felt I had to get away. I needed to be on my own for a bit. It's been such a long time since I was.

You moved when Grandad died, he says.

That's true, I say. He was my daddy in the same way that I'm your daddy and I didn't like him dying. I was upset.

Daddies mustn't die, Gregus says.

You're right, I say.

Nor Mummies, he says.

Agreed, I say.

But do you sort of dream when you're dead, he asks.

Afraid not, I say. No dreams. You simply don't exist any more.

Does it hurt?

No, I say. You don't feel anything. All animals and people and plants die when they get old. It's no big deal.

Will you and Mummy die? he asks.

Yes, we will, I say.

Will I go on living after you're dead? he asks.

Yes, I say.

You know, he says. I hope I die at the same time as you.

That's good that you feel like that, I say, but I think you'll see it differently when you grow up. We can come back to this later.

The lack of stimulation out here has a positive effect on Gregus. We sit by the fire for long periods and just chat and do nothing in particular. We can hear the faint drone from the town and the occasional whistle of a train. It sounds a little like the Canadian trains I've seen on TV. They're really long over there, I know, and the whistle-blasts sound portentous as they cover hundreds of miles through wasteland, from coast to coast. After a while we go out and try to teach Bongo to fetch sticks we throw, but he can't see the point, and to tell the truth neither can I, so we go back to the tent and continue to do nothing until we get bored. It's embedded in our DNA that we constantly have to be doing things. Finding things to do. As long as you're active that's fine, in a way, however mindless the activity. We want to avoid boredom at all costs, but I've started to notice that I like being bored. Boredom is underrated. I tell Gregus that my plan is to bore myself to happiness. I have no doubt that there is something that approximates satisfaction beyond boredom, but of course I do not expect Gregus to feel the same, so after a few more hours spent listlessly dozing and grilling meat we go out to find ourselves raw materials to make bows and arrows. The season is perhaps not the most suitable, but I've heard that ash is the best wood for a bow, so I chop down two branches of what I believe is ash but may well be a different tree, and since Gregus's patience will not allow us to let the wood dry out for a year, which is the ideal, we get cracking and remove the bark and carve grooves in the ends and make strings by plaiting sinews from Bongo's mother. I make arrows, too. Good ones with a point. And then we shoot wildly all around us. And upwards. That's what we both like best, we discover. We fire as high as we can and take care that we don't get any arrows in our heads when they return to the ground. It's wonderful when the arrows thwack a deep hole into the ground a few metres away. We pass the hours in this way until Gregus's body senses it's time for children's TV and twitches. Look, Daddy, he says, my arm's twitching. So it is, I say. Why do you think that is? Don't know, he says. Well, I certainly don't know, I say.

We fire off a few more arrows, but I can see that Gregus has completely lost his enthusiasm. His eyes are glassy and distant. He is struggling and I feel sorry for him.

It's children's TV, I say. That's why your arm's twitching. Your body's trying to tell you to turn on the television. I could feel there was something, Gregus says. But where's the TV? I don't have a TV, I explain. It's not normal to have a TV in the forest. But then can we go somewhere where there is a TV? Gregus asks. No, I say. You'll have to do without while you're here with me. I want to see children's TV, he says. No chance, I say. But I want to, he repeats, and I can see that he's on the point of losing control, so without any further ado I swing him onto Bongo's back and we charge down to Düsseldorf's house.

Düsseldorf is sitting over a model as usual, probably oblivious to the fact that we are seconds away from children's TV swooping in over our long and narrow country. I bang on his back door, explain the situation and ask if we can come in for three quarters of an hour to watch TV. Düsseldorf says that's fine. Bongo and Gregus step carefully over the model of the war-ravaged Belgian town and curl up on the sofa as the animated children's TV jingle rolls over the screen. Gregus hums along. I take a seat at the table with Düsseldorf. He's still building his German Steyr Type 1500A/01 and making the figure that will represent his father.

Looks like it's taking its time, I say.

The problem is more that it doesn't take enough time, Düsseldorf says. I've always been a finicky modeller, but I have attained a level of precision now that I've never even been near before. I'm together with my father when I do this. And when I've finished I can't be with him any more. I've noticed that actually I don't want to finish.

You could make some more, I say. You could make other war scenes. You could make the walks in the forest your mother and father took in Oslo.

No, Düsseldorf says. I know that I'll never make any more

 87

models after this, and within a couple of weeks at the most I'll have finished. I reckon I'll be finished by Christmas.

Perhaps you're investing too much of yourself into it, I say. After all, this is plastic models we're talking about.

I am not investing too much of myself into it, Düsseldorf says. Quite the opposite, I'm investing the exact significance and gravity it deserves. It's you who are not investing enough into it.

Possibly, I say.

And it's not plastic models we're talking about, he says. We're talking about the biggest war the world has ever seen. We're talking about tens of millions of dead and even more with permanent injuries, myself included. We're talking about Europe. Poor Europe. And about large parts of the rest of the world. Poor rest of the world. And then we're talking about my father. We're talking about him, Düsseldorf says, pointing to the tiny plastic soldier he has attached to a home-made stand under a large magnifying glass and which he is painting now in immense detail. The buttons on the uniform, the shirt sleeves barely poking out of the jacket, fingers, nails, everything in consistent naturalistic colours. Just the face is missing. Düsseldorf's father's face hasn't been painted yet and I realise that now it is its turn. I've as good as decided that he'll be smiling, Düsseldorf says. It hasn't been an easy decision to make because there are several factors to suggest that he would not be smiling that day, but I still think he's smiling as he drives through the town on his way to deliver a report to General Manteuffel, and he's smiling because he's thinking about his son, in other words me. He's only seen me in a photograph, but he knows that I exist, and the fact that I exist makes him put on a tentative smile, to himself. It's important that it shouldn't be an unqualified beam because that doesn't tie in with his circumstances. But nor must it be an inscrutable Mona Lisa-like grimace, which might mean anything. The teeth mustn't show, but there shouldn't be any doubt that he's smiling, Düsseldorf says. He should be thinking that I'm learning to walk and feeling confident that the war will soon be over. As the sniper fires he should be sitting in the car and looking forward to seeing me.

Düsseldorf says all of this while applying a primary coat to his father's face and without looking up.

I see, I say. That sounds like a good idea.

I'm not sure if it's a good idea, Düsseldorf says, but that's the way it's going to be anyway.

Mm, I say and I notice a pile of empty pizza boxes on the kitchen worktop, and I assume that cooking is not high on the agenda in the Düsseldorf home during the day. By the way, have you had any dinner?

No dinner, says Düsseldorf.

Shall I make you some? I ask.

Thank you for offering, he says, but the only thing that tastes of anything at the moment is pizza, so if you want to ring for one, that would be kind of you. I don't like to interrupt my work for anything so trivial. The telephone number's on the fridge. Order the one with pepperoni and garlic, but without pineapple. I've never understood what pineapples have got to do with pizzas. It's a rotten combination. And order one for yourselves if you fancy one.

I glance over at the sofa where both Gregus and Bongo have fallen asleep entwined, with the light from the TV news flickering over them. They had enjoyed the pleasurable part of the evening's viewing and fell asleep to all the misery that was now washing over them.

I think we should be heading home, I say, going into the kitchen and ordering Düsseldorf's pizza.

Thereafter I wake Bongo gently and lead him into the garden before carefully carrying Gregus out and placing him on Bongo's back.

What are you doing for Christmas? Düsseldorf asks when I go back to thank him.

For Christmas I'm doing absolutely nothing, I say.

Then you might be interested in having a simple meal here with me on Christmas Eve, he says.

Not impossible, I say.

Let's say it's a deal then, Düsseldorf says, waving us off.

And in biblical fashion we make our way up to the tent. I place my jacket over Gregus and think I'm managing pretty well as a father despite the long break. That's what I think.

As I hand over Gregus next day Nora thrusts a print-out into my hands from a website called The Elvish Name Generator.

She's entered my name, Andreas Doppler, and with the help of Tolkien's I'm sure highly intricate and accurate linguistic logic the program has worked out that my elf name is Valandil Tîwele.

It sounds clearly Elvish, and I say thank you and ask if there is anything special she's trying to say by giving me this. She shakes her head. She just wanted me to know, she says. She wanted me to keep at the back of mind that I have an elf name.

Fine, I say. I'll certainly keep it at the back of my mind.

Afterwards I take my leave of Nora, Gregus and my wife who, by the way, had a fantastic long weekend in Rome. She revelled in classical culture and shopped for clothes and accessories, which obviously restored some of her sparkle. It's astonishing to observe how much clothes and accessories can mean. A new accessory at the right moment can make all the difference. May God bless objects. My wife beams and twitters and for that reason I return to the forest in the dusk almost without a bad conscience. Gregus would have preferred to continue living with me in the tent, I know, but he can forget that. The forest is mine and I have to be alone there if I'm going to achieve what I want, I reflect, even though I'm not quite sure what it is I want.

You can have him for a bit at weekends, can't you? my wife says.

In the forest there's no difference between weekend and workdays, I say, so the answer's no, or rather, nothing doing.

I'll go up to the tent with him, she says.

Then you'll have to be prepared for an arrow through the neck, I say.

I struggle to maintain motivation for a few days. I sit idly by the fire whittling away at arrows and wondering what I'm doing up there in the forest. From time to time I gently tousle Bongo's coat and hum without enthusiasm. Going down to the house and being with Gregus has disrupted the good rhythm I had established. Now I'm out of balance again. I reflect that I've come a long way from where I was before the forest embraced me, if I can express myself like that. It's pompous but nonetheless quite true. I was in all the usual places and did the usual things that people in Oslo do, and then all of a sudden the forest opened its arms and embraced me. It adopted me. And it was about time. I can see that now. I was becoming spiteful and annoying to those around me. I wasn't the sort of person that Oslo would want to have in its streets. I didn't radiate positive energy. I wasn't a benefit to anyone. Neither to those nearest to me, nor my job nor the more diffuse greater society around me, nor the economic framework that governs it. I was becoming a burden, and then I was excluded. Nature is set up so ingeniously that it excluded me before I did any real damage. It's an impressive system. Millennia of nature and culture have refined the mechanism in such a way that the likes of me are removed from the ranks. We are rendered harmless. Enemies of the people who are about to smash the fragile illusion of community and meaning are sent away to have another think. To sea, for example, or to the mountains, or behind some locked door, or as in my case: into the forest. It's a cunning form of punishment which feels like a kind of reward at the same time.

This and more I think, sitting by the fire.

I have no idea to what extent these thoughts are rooted in reality. Nor if what we so boldly call reality exists at all. The only thing I can be fairly sure about is that the fire warms me and that a little elk by the name of Bongo lies at my feet purring, if that's what you call it when elk emit sounds of pleasure.

And Christmas is upon us.

I can sense it because the afternoon is quieter than is normally the case. The population down in Oslo stops moving. They have arrived at the places where they are going to spend the next hours and that's where they stay. I suppose this happens on only this one day of the year. And when it happens less noise reaches the forest from Oslo. The town becomes gentler, in a way. It becomes innocuous and tame. It eats from my hand. And then come the church bells. Ringing out of synch. Gradually they are attuned into one another and Bongo and I take the opportunity to exchange gifts. He gets a nice little hat that I made myself from crepe paper. It was sticking out of a rubbish bin a few days ago when I

93

chanced by, as they say, and so I took it with me and later spent a few hours at night folding it into a cleverly designed hat. As for me, I don't get a great deal. In fact, I get nothing at all, but my God, Bongo is an elk, I don't doubt for a second that I would have got a terrific present if he'd understood what Christmas was. You're a present in yourself, you are, Bongo, I say. Don't worry your head about it. My present is you being here with me. And Merry Christmas.

When Düsseldorf opens the door to us I notice that he has enormous bags under his eyes and is wearing the same clothes I saw him in two weeks before.

Oh sod it, it's Christmas, is the first thing he says.

He's forgotten all about the Christmas dinner, but invites us in anyway, very embarrassed. He directs us to the sofa and nips down to the freezer and finds some cloudberries which he throws into the convector oven without taking them out of the bag. Then he hurriedly takes a seat at the piano and tries to cheer us, and himself, up with a few verses of a Christmas hymn, 'Beauty Around Us', but it's just a mess.

I think perhaps we should go so that you can continue with the model, I say after a short time.

Do you really think so? Düsseldorf says, visibly relieved.

Yes, I say. You seem to have been very preoccupied with something.

Funny you should say that, he says, because that's just what I was. It's my father's face. I think I'm onto something.

94

I'm getting close. I've got the smile, and now it's the eyes.

We both go over to the table where the stand holding the small plastic soldier is in the same position as before. There's a photograph of his father beside it and it's easy to see that Düsseldorf's right when he says he's onto something. There's a frightening similarity between the figure and the man in the photograph.

I'm speechless, I say.

Mm, says Düsseldorf. There's not a lot to say.

I'm sorry about the dinner, he says. We could try again on New Year's Eve.

Don't worry, I say. There will be more Christmases.

Let's hope so, Düsseldorf says.

On the way out I take the cloudberries with me, more frozen than thawed. Düsseldorf has enough presence of mind to tie a red ribbon around the freezer bag so that it doesn't look so unlike a kind of gift.

Thank you, I say. And Merry Christmas.

Thank you and the same to you, Düsseldorf says.

Approaching the tent, I see that Toolman Roger has dropped by with a gift. He's written a note to thank me for the DVD player and the DVDs. His kids were really pleased with them, he writes. I unwrap the present and find a picklock and have to swallow a couple of times. That's what I call a pal. The rest of the day is spent slurping half-frozen cloudberries. Bongo goes to sleep early and I sit by the fire for a long time thinking that Düsseldorf sets an excellent example when it comes to honouring your father. My father ought to be honoured like that. Even though I didn't know him. Or perhaps precisely because I didn't know him. He went through life doing what he wanted. The same way I do. He was just there. As I am also just here.

If I don't honour my father, no one will. I'm going to make a totem pole in his memory. Suddenly it's all very clear to me that this may be the only right thing to do. I'll carve it with my own hands and erect it here in the forest. I fall asleep as, in my mind's eye, I rough out what a totem pole of this kind should look like.

Over Christmas we stay in a lot of the time. It's cold and unpleasant outside and the snow is still overdue. For the most part I sit in front of the fire whittling objects that fifty or a hundred years ago I could have sold in the town market during the summer, but today you can buy them for next to nothing in IKEA. Mass production has knocked the bottom out of the barter economy. It laughs at people like me. But I'm not going to give in. I keep whittling, and every now and then I try to teach Bongo a few simple words, but before long I realise that he hasn't a hope. He can manage the occasional vowel if we're not too strict about the articulation but he's nowhere near pronouncing the consonants. You've got a long way to go, you have, Bongo, I say. No doubt about that. But I'll be with you every step. You can be sure of that. I'll be with you every step of the way.

On New Year's Eve Düsseldorf hasn't progressed much from where he was on Christmas Eve. The difference this time is that he knows it and on the doorstep he has placed a bottle of vodka with a red bow round. I'm getting there, it says on a card painted by mouth and foot artists. And Happy New Year. I take the hint and don't knock, but I grab the bottle and head for the tent, where I drink myself senseless before going out to the pissing place and surveying Oslo, thinking that my resolutions for the New Year are to build a totem pole in memory of my father and otherwise do as little as humanly possible. I'm going to cultivate doing nothing to a level few have achieved before me. And I'm not going to return to civilisation, not bloody likely. And since I'm there I start shouting. I'm the King and the Prime Minister and I hold a speech to the nation. My dear compatriots, I shout, I don't like you. Pull yourselves together. Raise your sights and stop being so bloody smug. And, you right-wingers, get rid of your sodding dogs and wipe off those self-satisfied smiles of yours, and start bartering. And cycling. We have to cycle and barter like buggery if we're going to have any chance of surviving. And who owns the wind rustling in the trees and the flowers in the field? And may the Teletubbies burn in hell, and shit, I come to a halt, I'm too drunk to retain my train of thought through a New Year's speech, but Løvenskiold, I shout, you give the forest back to the people because actually you don't own it, no one should be able to own a forest, and Dad, I

97

continue, you've gone and I didn't know you and I feel alone, I've always felt alone and I push everyone away because I'm a prat like everyone else, and no one knows me and I fear no one will ever know me for as long as I live, and I give up and in the end I just shout shit, shit, shit until I lose my voice.

Poor Bongo doesn't recognise me. It's irresponsible of me to drink so much with a youngster like him nearby. After all, I'm his guardian and I'm setting an embarrassingly bad example. But it does me good to shout. So I continue to drink and shout and rave incoherently and I'm aware that right now for Bongo I must be behaving like the decibel scale. Ten minutes with me in this condition can just about be tolerated, but twenty minutes doesn't mean a doubling of the effect, as you might believe, but a hundred times more, and thirty minutes is a thousand times more. That's how decibels behave. And that's how I behave as we enter the New Year. A New Year with niceness and devilry and belief and hope and love in the world.

But the greatest of all is the forest.

january

There's not much to say about January.

It's dark and it's cold and I stoke the fire like a madman to keep warm.

One of the first things I do in the New Year is to renew the milk agreement. I wrap up a large piece of meat and leave it where I usually collect the milk. In many ways the milk is the foundation stone on which the fragile edifice of Doppler rests. Without milk he, I that is, is as good as nothing. But now I'm approaching a milk-rich time, and as long as there is skimmed milk there is hope.

Straight after New Year huge amounts of snow fall and this makes me less grumpy than for a long time. I fetch my skis from the garage at home and I spend several days criss-crossing the landscape to find a suitable trunk as a totem pole. Bongo jogs along after me, thinking snow is fun even if it's harder for him to move about.

One beautiful night the almost four-metre-long tent pole breaks. It's about zero degrees outside, it has started to snow like crazy after we fall asleep and it seems the tent is not designed for these conditions. Bongo and I wake up with the tent canvas weighing heavily on us and I flounder around looking for the opening and crawl out. I remove the snow from the tent, cut myself a new pole from the undergrowth and erect the tent once again. After recovering from the shock, building up the fire and chatting long enough for us to feel debriefed and calm, we both fall asleep again.

Eventually I find a suitable tree for the totem pole. But it's quite a distance from the tent. I chop it down, and using Bongo as a draught elk I spend almost ten days dragging it back home to the camp. Bongo is completely exhausted, the poor thing. He loses a lot of weight and at night I ski down to the farms in Maridalen and fill my sack with hay for him. He is insatiable. According to the elk calendar, he's on the cusp of becoming a teenager, I would guess. This is a sensitive and defiant period, and we have many long discussions about it. Bongo leaves the tent in a temper several times, but happily he always comes back.

On one of the trips to Maridalen I pick up a couple of good axes. I already have one of course, but these are almost brand new. They are sturdy Fiskars axes. And specially designed for forestry work, as far as I can judge. One of them is large and the other small, and I suppose the poor farmer must have been given them for Christmas. But that's life. It's give and take. I haven't ruled out the possibility that I might give them back when the totem pole is finished, though.

On the last day of January I realise that it's over a month since I've spoken to another human. No problem there. All the things we can say to others, and yet I haven't said anything. I'm living proof that there's basically not much to say. I'm proud of myself.

It's a good start to the year.

february

I spend a whole day enthusiastically humming a melody I can't place. I'm feeling on top of the world as I cheerfully chip away at the bark on the totem pole. Bits fly off into the forest as I work my way round the trunk, lost in my own world, humming and whistling all the while. Snatches of the lyrics begin to emerge by the evening, and I sing them uncritically for quite a time before I realise, in a cold sweat, that what I'm churning out is the signature tune to an Australian TV show, *Bananas in Pyjamas*. Not even out here in the forest am I spared the poisoned darts of children's culture. It's like a disease. You contract it through hearing. Even mild exposure to the source is sufficient to allow the virus to attack the brain without mercy. It can lie there quietly incubating for months while you go about your own business, not bothering anyone, and then suddenly it rears its ugly head. For the rest of the night it's like a running battle between me and *Bananas in Pyjamas*. I try to keep the song out, but back it comes. As soon as I lower my defences, I hum it again. It's like an obsession. It's like a film I saw many years ago where the main character's hand turns evil and tries to kill him. In the end, he cuts it off with a chain saw. He holds the chain saw in his healthy hand and pulls the starting cord with his mouth. Off with the evil arm.

I use bits of charcoal to draw the motif on the totem pole. At the bottom I leave a couple of metres' space as I'm going to dig it in later. Then above the ground there should be a base of about half a metre and after that there'll be an approximately two-metre high egg, actually a rhythm egg shaker, but you wouldn't be able to see that with the naked eye unless you knew my father, and nobody did, which I think I've already mentioned. So you wouldn't be able to see what it was. A casual passer-by would think it was an ordinary egg and that's alright by me. My father will be sitting on top of this egg shaker with his legs up under his chin and his arms out to the sides, and I'll be sitting on my father's head. On my bike. I get this idea while I'm drawing. It comes to me out of the ether, a wonderful inspiration, and I think, why not? I'll damn well carve myself a figure that's a representation of me sitting on my bike on top of my father. That would be so beautiful. And then on my head I'll have a miniature of Bongo standing erect and surveying the town. He deserves that after dragging this monster of a tree trunk up to the camp. He would have deserved it in any case. Simply because he's Bongo. But after he's quite literally invested kilos of himself in getting the totem pole up here, incorporating him in the work is no longer just a possibility, it's a necessity.

Two metres under the ground plus a plinth of half a metre

plus two metres of egg shaker plus four metres of Dad plus two metres of me on my bike plus Bongo. We're talking eleven metres of totem pole here, of which nine are above the ground. I'm in business.

Since this is my first totem pole I've no realistic idea how long it will take to carve. To begin with, I reckon it will take a few days, a couple of weeks at most, but as time passes I start extending my estimate and soon realise that it will take all winter and spring. The axes from Maridalen will be my closest companions during this period. I use one of them for rough hacking and the other for the more delicate work. Eventually I suppose I'll also need some chisels and a file and, doubtless, a not insubstantial amount of sandpaper. Bongo is no help whatsoever in this process. He wanders around me restlessly as I chip away. I try to explain to him that he's already done his bit. I would never have got this tree to the camp without you, I say. You're one of the most important players in the game, and it's not your fault that you're an elk and can't use tools. You missed the boat millions of years ago. That happened when some representatives of our common origins broke with one another and went their separate ways. Those who were to be my ancestors went in the direction of the fascinating world of tools and fine motor skills, and those who were to become your ancestors made a different choice. And that was that. In hindsight, you might say that they should have given it more thought, but it wasn't so easy to know, and in spite of everything, in my opinion, under the circumstances, you elk are doing alright. In my opinion, things have turned out well for you despite the pretty sorry start. But Bongo doesn't want to know. He finds it boring with me chipping away all day and he wants some attention. He springs up onto the totem pole and leaps down again, careering around in a spectacular, foolhardy manner. And he runs head first at trees trying to break them. Pull yourself together, Bongo, I say. I quite understand that you consider this boring, but I have to honour my father and you have to accept that. You can honour your own father and mother if you want. I won't stand in your way. But I must warn you against practising the kind of extreme sport of which I've seen signs just now. It will all end in tears or maybe something even worse. Have you any idea how many elk come to grief in bogs or fall off steep precipices every year through downright carelessness? You've got this one chance, I say. I don't know what you elk believe in, but I can tell you that if that mother of yours deluded you into imagining there's a life after death, then you can just forget it. It's all lies. You are here now and you'll never be here again. And it's not cool being dead. Don't ever forget that.

After three weeks I have carved out the plinth and the egg shaker and they do actually resemble a plinth and an egg. I'm rather proud of myself, even if I say so myself. I'm not the most experienced wielder of an axe in this world, but somehow I've still managed. Every evening in the tent I fall asleep from exhaustion, after having had my fill of Bongo's mother, who is holding up quite well.

Bongo has begun to go for walks on his own. He usually hangs around the camp for the first few hours after breakfast, but then he heads off and seldom returns before nightfall. What he gets up to, I've no idea, but I presume it's the usual elk things and nothing I need worry about. I suppose he has a need to be on his own a little, as indeed I have. I imagine he's subject to the contradictory forces of the teenage years tearing at his soul, veering from one extreme to the other several times a day: from the soft to the hard, the poetic to the vulgar. And, naturally, there will be questions about things with which I can't really help him. I can give him a secure base and the certainty that he's loved, but he has to go out into the world himself. In fact, it is harsh out there. Even for elk.

One evening after work I went with Bongo to see how Düsseldorf was getting on. To be honest, I was a bit worried. When I saw him at Christmas he had already reached a stage in his obsession where you began to wonder just how healthy this all was for him. A positive outcome was by no means a foregone conclusion. But now, as he opens the door, I can see that a lot has happened, and whatever it is that has happened has the potential to surprise me. I can hardly recognise him. He is well-groomed and nicely dressed, and the house is immaculate. The village from 1944 is still spread out on the living-room floor, but the table with all the model-building paraphernalia has been cleared. He receives us with warmth and serves dinner in the twinkling of an eye.

You're looking good, I say.

Thank you very much, Düsseldorf says.

Did you finish your father? I ask.

My father? he asks, as though it were strange of me to mention him at all.

You were painting his face, I say.

Oh, that, Düsseldorf says. Funny you should remember that. I put all that behind me a long time ago.

This reply makes me slightly uneasy. I'm no expert on the human mind and its labyrinths, but now a little alarm bell is ringing, I can hear.

What happened? I ask.

Düsseldorf doesn't answer. He leans back in his Stressless chair and his mind wanders.

Maybe we should talk about something else, he says. It seems so long ago. I don't know how relevant it is any longer.

It's relevant, I say.

OK, OK, he says. If you say so.

He closes his eyes and appears to be concentrating.

I finished, he says. I finished painting my father's face. It took me a long time. But it looked just like him. It was him, in a way. And when it had become completely him I put him in the car and placed him in the street. Düsseldorf nods in the direction of the huge model of the village laid out on the floor. I turn towards the living room to have a look, and sure enough there is his father sitting in the car. He's approaching the fateful crossroads, and the clock on the town hall tower shows it's approaching twenty past two. It's going to happen and it has happened. It is, in fact, an impressively pleasing and detailed image. I admire what Düsseldorf has done for his father. But it seems it might have cost him some of his sanity.

What else? I ask

What do you mean? Düsseldorf asks.

What else did you do? I ask.

He hesitates before replying.

I tossed things around in my head for a while, he says. But finally I went and got my shotgun. And then I loaded it and lay on the sofa and stuck the end of the barrel in my mouth, but I didn't pull the trigger. I thought why all the hurry, and then I thought I might just as well switch on the TV, as the remote was close at hand, I could switch channels and everything without taking the barrel out of my mouth. I saw the whole of the news lying like that, and it must have been a Friday because right after the news came *Norway Countrywide,* and it had been a long time since I'd seen *Norway Countrywide,* so I watched that, too. Do you watch *Norway Countrywide*? he asks me.

Now and then, I say. But it's quite a while since I have.

People ought to watch *Norway Countrywide,* says Düsseldorf.

Very true, I say. It's a good local affairs programme.

It's about us people, says Düsseldorf. It's about you and me.

That's right, I say. It's about Norwegian people. And about Norwegian animals, too, for that matter. In fact, maybe it's especially about the interaction between Norwegian people and Norwegian animals.

But it's friendly, Düsseldorf says. It's a friendly programme.

Was there anything in particular that made an impression on you? I ask.

Düsseldorf silently nods his head.

There were two things, he says. First there was something about a Finnish woman who, in her youth, had worked as a nurse somewhere in southern Finland. On her first holiday she decided to hitch-hike to the north to look at a church she had seen a picture of in one of her school books when she was a child. That church had stuck in her mind. She thought it was beautiful and she wanted to see it, so she set off hitching. She was advised to take a bus for the last stretch and for a long time she was the only passenger on the bus, but then along came a young Norwegian and he asked if he could sit next to her. Even though the bus was virtually empty, he asked if he could sit down beside her. And they began to talk and one thing led to another and she dropped the visit to the church and went back with him to his home in Finnmark where they got married and had children and all that kind of thing, and fifty years passed. In the story on

TV she took the bus back to see the Finnish church. She was so happy to be able to go there. She had her husband with her. Both of them were still alive and they were so fond of each other and at last she got to see the church that had held such an attraction for her and which was the reason why her life had turned out the way it did. I don't know why it made such an impression on me, says Düsseldorf, trying to pretend that there weren't any small tears running down his cheek.

You'd been working too hard, I said. You were worn to a frazzle.

Yes, says Düsseldorf. But even so.

I know what he means. There can be something reconciling about a good story on *Norway Countrywide*. If you're in the right frame of mind you can become attached to those people struggling with their problems, and who are pleasant, and helpless. And, not only that, the programme tells you that it's fine to be different, as long as you're also Norwegian. We're Norwegian and different, all of us. And since everybody is different, in a way it's normal to be different, so the conclusion must be that none of us is different. Just Norwegian.

And the other thing? I ask.

There was a young man from Vestland, he says. He had learned virtually all the national anthems in the world all on his own. And there was something unsettling about it all, but the people around him accepted him and thought he was clever. His classmates drew scraps of paper out of a cup and on them were written the names of various countries whose anthems he then performed, in the original language, and moreover in quite a different, and therefore especially moving voice. That young man decided me to take the barrel out of my mouth and the cartridge out of the chamber, Düsseldorf says. And ever since, I've just looked to the future. Dad can fend for himself. I've finished with him. One of these days I'm going to clear away the whole village. I've had enough. And I'm actually wondering whether to ring that man up and ask him if he would be interested in taking a cruise up the western coast with me this summer. Then we could have a closer look at this elongated country of ours, and I could get to learn some good national anthems. It feels like it's an opportunity I shouldn't pass up.

You know what will happen if I ring *Norway Countrywide* and tell them about you? I say.

Düsseldorf shakes his head and looks at me, eyes agog. They'll be out here like bats out of hell, I say. They'll come with blue lights flashing. It's perfect TV material. Son of a German soldier who didn't have the easiest start in life and has now spent years constructing a model of the Belgian village at the time when his father was shot during the Ardennes offensive in 1944, a model which is so accurate as to be verging on the mentally insane, and who on top of that, in his darkest hour, is saved by a *Norway Countrywide* story, and then ends up in beautiful Norwegian cruise-liner landscape with a former *Norway Countrywide* star. That's as good as it gets. And if you can slip in that a friend of yours who lives in the forest with his elk occasionally drops by, then it's a prize at Montreux and all the other TV awards ceremonies festivals, but that won't happen, I say, because Bongo and I don't want to be on TV, but you might very well be, and if you want I can give them a ring.

Can you? Düsseldorf says.

If that's what you yourself want, I say.

I think maybe I do, he says.

Then I'll ring, I say, getting to my feet. I find the number in the directory and ask the NRK switchboard to put me through to *Norway Countrywide*. There I leave a message informing them who Düsseldorf is and what he has done that might be of interest to them and tell them where they can contact him when they get to work next morning. I don't lay it on thick, just present it as it is; from my own experience I know that short and sweet always works best when it comes to the crunch and that the fine folk who work at *Norway Countrywide* are sure to know that perfectly well.

I carry on carving. Now it's my father's turn. I soon give up any idea of creating a close resemblance between my father's actual appearance and my totem pole representation of him. It will be a stylised and simplified version of my father, but of course it's the symbolism that counts here. He'll also be considerably larger than he was in real life. Four metres in sitting position would correspond to about eight metres standing, I would think, and my father was nowhere near that size. He was average height, not physically striking in any way. I am enlarging him, one might say. I'm making him bigger than he was.

One morning while we're having breakfast, I hear sounds near the tent. I peer out and see a dog I recognise. It's Reactionary Dog, and, quick as a flash, I work out that the reactionary can't be far away. I grab my bow and a good arrow and squat down on my haunches in the tent opening. Eventually I see his shape looming in the undergrowth. He's skiing and has donned his Sunday breeches, even though it isn't Sunday, and he's carrying a fairly voluminous rucksack on his back.

Halt, Reactionary Man! I shout, drawing my bow.

He raises his arm and says something I don't catch, but which I later learn was: I come in peace. But, as I say, I don't catch it and therefore choose to interpret it as a threat that before very long he will be ringing his friend Løvenskiold, notifying him about my trespassing and telling Løvenskiold to send in his henchmen to pull down my tent and kick me out of the forest. And that must not happen. I can't accept that. I'm raising a totem pole in honour of my father and I have to protect both my own and my father's interests. I draw the bow and again tell him to stop, but he doesn't.

Now you're for it, I shout and let fly with an arrow. Unfortunately, I can say now in hindsight. It wasn't a very wise thing to have done. For the arrow is sticking out of the reactionary's thigh, and he falls to the ground. It's easy to be wise after the event, of course I shouldn't have done it, but I was scared and had been provoked and therefore made a mistake. It's not uncommon for people to do that sort of thing. It's happened before and it will happen again. The slightest complaint to Løvenskiold and I would have had to leave my beloved forest, and Bongo, and the totem pole, forever, and I couldn't bear the thought of that, so I let fly at him. In any case I never thought I would hit him. But I hit him smack in the thigh. He's lying in the snow, writhing about down in the undergrowth. Is it my problem? I ask myself, and soon realise that yes, indeed it is, so I run through the deep snow and make contact.

I'm very sorry, I say. But I didn't think I would hit you. He's not in any condition to talk to or forgive anyone. He just lies there in the snow groaning, stunned and annoyed. I remove his rucksack and drag him back with me to the tent and lay him in front of the fire. There I pull out the arrow, clean the wound with vodka and dress it with strips of cloth I tear off a shirt. The reactionary says nothing and eventually falls asleep, and I go out to continue my carving, while Bongo and the reactionary dog get chummy. I like the unsentimental manner in which I have tackled the situation. By rights I suppose I should have called in the health authorities, but I can sense I'm planning to try to persuade him to let it remain an issue between him and me. There would soon be complications if I lifted him onto Bongo's back and went down to the Rikshospital. Down there they would start asking questions, and the upshot might be that my anonymous forest existence would be compromised. Maybe the forces of law and order would also get wind of the incident and, even though this can't be the first time someone has been unfortunate enough to shoot a reactionary in the thigh, deep down I know I won't be met by a sympathetic response with them. Fortunately, however, we are mature individuals who I am sure can resolve our differences once the reactionary has had some sleep and gathered his thoughts.

Late that evening he wakes up, proffers his hand and introduces himself as Bosse Munch. Bosse, I say, savouring the word. It's got a bloody nice ring to it. It must be part of the right-wing conspiracy, I fancy. They give the right-wing children pleasant-sounding names so that it's easy to like them throughout their lives, in spite of their bizarre opinions and all their money. I give Bosse some water and elk meat while I clean his wound once more. It's not as bad as I first feared. The wound is not very deep, and it doesn't seem as if any of the vital nerves or organs have been affected. He can move all his toes and joints in the vicinity of the wound without any trouble. In other words, it was a perfect warning shot. I put the wind up him, but he won't suffer any permanent damage.

I didn't come to ask you to move the tent, Bosse says when he has had a little to eat and drink. I came because I've been doing a lot of thinking in the couple of months since I was last here.

Oh yes, I say.

For the first few days after you shouted at me I was furious and I was on the point of ringing Carl-Otto several times and getting him to demand that you remove the tent, he says. But as time went by I came to my senses and in the end I could feel myself agreeing with you. You and everyone else should have an undisputed right to take up residence in the forest, if you feel the need for it, for however long.

I'm glad you see it that way, I say.

I'm glad you're glad, says Bosse. But it doesn't stop there. What you said about material security and my self-satisfied smirk made me see the error of my ways and realise that it was time to change. The kids flew the coop long ago of course and I can tell you without a word of a lie that my many directorships are just a question of marking time. The proposals from the various managing directors are accepted without question and at the board dinners, for ten or fifteen years now, we have been saying more or less the same things to each other as we have said hundreds of times before. So, to cut a long story short, I tried to get my wife to agree to us selling the house and giving some of the money away and finding something completely different to do, but she didn't think that was a very good idea. She's spread roots, as she puts it. We have a lovely garden, and the view, and what with one thing and another, she didn't want to. But as the weeks passed

 121

I felt that I wasn't finding any peace with this, and this morning I got the idea into my head that I should move out here for a while. Close to you, I thought. So that we could have a bit of a chat, maybe, and generally support each other in various ways, I imagined. I don't know what you think to that.

Mmm, I say. Actually I settled here to get away from people a bit, so I'm afraid the quality of my project will deteriorate somewhat if our numbers out here increase. But, on the other hand, I can't prevent you from being here, of course. It's your forest just as much as it's mine.

Yes, that's true, Bosse says, sleepily reclining on the mat.

My forest, he says in his dreams as he nods off again.

After Bosse has fallen asleep I strap on skis and go off on a long tour to ponder the new situation. Can't I even be on my own in the forest? A confused soul-searching reactionary is the last thing I need. On I go, thinking like this and getting worked up, when I meet the fifth jogger with a lamp on his forehead, and I explode. I push him into the snow and tear the lamp off his forehead, together with the absurdly heavy combi-battery pack. He has enough power to go to the North Cape, floodlit all the way. What the hell is this? I yell. What kind of a society is it we live in when a man can't even go for an evening constitutional to turn things over in his mind without being disturbed by people tearing through the forest with lamps on their heads? I can see the tracks and the trees perfectly clearly myself. Surely you can understand that this is bound to come to a sticky end, I say. The jogger nods meekly. And that I'm going to have to confiscate this lamp as well, I say. He nods again. Good, I say. And I don't want to see you out here with one of these lamps again. And I don't like you running so fast, either. You'll have to slow down a bit from now on. Have we got a deal? He confirms that we have. After that I help him to his feet and brush off a little snow here and there before sending him on his way with a friendly pat on the shoulder.

If you explain to folk why what they are doing is wrong, in an unthreatening manner, then they take heed. That's a redeeming feature, no question. Good, old-fashioned conversation is not dead yet. And in a way it is especially good in the forest.

march

It's beginning to get crowded in the forest.

This new trend is unfortunate, to put it mildly.

I gave the reactionary the big E after a few days and expected him to trudge home again, but I was wrong. He has lived for several weeks now in a small mountain tent only a couple of hundred metres away. He's settled in and there's not much I can do about it. I've decided to continue thinking of him as the reactionary and not as Bosse. I like the distance that creates. I need that. Sadly, his wound has healed so well that he's forever dropping in. Any old excuse will do to come over and visit me. An unending stream of things he wants to borrow, salt, knives and all sorts of odds and ends. But I've put my foot down and told him not to come more than two or three times a week. I can't face any more than that. After all, he's not exactly stimulating company. But he doesn't take any notice. He pops by several times a day and has a great need to talk. Especially about how he has suddenly seen the light, in all its clarity, and how he's wasted a large part of his life on trivialities, but now he's planning to make amends. Amongst other things, he's planning a reconciliation festival, as he calls it. I'm not quite sure what this is all about, it seems he's going to invite representatives of various religions to a kind of party under the banner of brotherhood. He asked me whether I was interested in taking part, but I said forget it.

It's become far more difficult to do things, and it's become impossible to do nothing. Doing nothing is a very demanding job when other people are constantly on your back. It's come to the point now where I'll have to explain myself. I will have to make my position clear with regard to another person's wishes. I'll have to explain that I don't want any visits. I'll have to explain that I don't like him and that it would suit me best if he moved back home. It's draining me. I'm beginning to see how much easier it is not to explain anything, not to say anything, and just keep going about my business as usual. I don't know what to do. One option, of course, would be to move farther into the forest. Take the tent and all my other stuff and one quiet night slip into the farthest depths of the forest. That would probably be the right thing to do, but I'm still hoping that the reactionary will call it a day and go back home. I try my best to freeze him out by being even more unfriendly towards him than I otherwise would have been. It's not that I like him any less than other people I don't like, not deep down. I just don't like him in a very general, indifferent sort of way. There's nothing special about him. But now I'm focussing on not liking him, so that it will become apparent even to him, who, as I see it, hasn't spent a lot of time in environments where people are particularly sensitive to the signals others send. But even though I treat him badly he keeps coming back. He wants to play lotto. He wants to do that every evening. He says there has been far too little fun or play in his life. When he was small, it was all about growing up, and when his children were small he was anywhere but at home, he was creating a name for himself and making money, and all that stuff.

You reap what you sow, I say.

He considers us friends and looks up to me in a disquieting way. I sense an expectation in him that I'll be a kind of mentor to him.

I can't imagine anything I'm less cut out to do.

I couldn't be a mentor to anybody. Not even myself. Ending up here in the forest was in many ways more a stroke of good fortune than any act of astuteness on my part. I fell off my bike at the right place and the right time.

But the reactionary regards me as some kind of soothsayer. He doesn't notice that I'm actually trying to get him to go home. I'm too soft-hearted.

A typical conversation with the reactionary tends to spread over several days and may develop like this:

Day 1:

I might be working on the totem pole. He mooches up and stands next to me. I say nothing. Just keep chipping away. He watches what I'm doing for a while before he says something.

Yo, Doppler, he says at length, what positive qualities can you see in me? If you had to name a few to a priest, say, who had to give a little speech at my funeral or something, the reactionary asks.

I take a little break from what I'm doing, think about how to answer and how to get rid of him as quickly as possible.

I don't know you, I say. But based on the little I've seen, I can't see any positive qualities in you.

None? the reactionary asks.

Well, I say. I suppose you took it pretty well when the arrow got you in the thigh, and also coming out here to live in the forest is possibly a positive quality in itself, but choosing this particular part of the forest loses you points, so all in all you don't come off that well there either.

He thinks about this a bit, then walks off to his tent.

Day 2:

Same situation. I'm chopping away and he turns up.

I've been thinking a lot about what you said yesterday, he says. About me not having any positive qualities. And I think you're right. I haven't any positive qualities. I'm a nothing. I've wasted my life.

Easy now, I say. You're down in the dumps at the moment. That's all. I'm sure you've got loads of unique qualities and talents and all that. But perhaps the forest is not the best showcase for all those fine attributes you have inside you.

He walks off to his tent.

Day 3:

I'm eating lunch and he comes over earlier than usual, silky-smooth.

I've been thinking about what you said yesterday, he says. About my unique qualities and talents and all that. You're right. I am unique and talented. And you're unique, too. We're both unique. Everyone is unique.

In a way, I say. But unique just means unique. It doesn't mean good.

Day 4:

He turns up as I'm having a piss.

I've been thinking about what you said about unique not necessarily meaning good, he says.

I carry on pissing.

You're right, he says. It's not much good being unique if you don't do what's right.

There's no such thing as right and wrong, as such, I say. It depends on who you are and when.

He leaves but comes back again after an hour.

I've been thinking about what you said about there being no such thing as right or wrong, as such, he says. And I believe you're right. I believe it all depends on the situation.

On and on he goes. The poor wretch is at a low ebb. I don't know how I can help him. He distracts me and he irritates me a lot. At the same time I feel sorry for him. The poor reactionary voter has spent all his life accumulating worldly goods and chattels and preserving the status quo, then all of a sudden he breaks down and no one in his clique is aware of it and comes to his aid. It's like landing back in teenagerhood after a long life. You don't recognise yourself any more. Your

131

body feels alien and scary. All the things you're used to being and having seem repulsive, and you can't just snap your fingers and change into someone else, for once you've played your hand, you've played your hand, that's it. It's truer than you think. That bloody hand. And I'm in the same boat myself, even though I might not appear quite as pitiful as the reactionary. But who knows?

But then it doesn't matter anyway.

Unfortunately, though, the reactionary is not the only disruptive element. Gregus is back. He's been here a couple of weeks. He legged it from the nursery and was observed approaching the outskirts of the forest. After making his way through more than a kilometre of residential housing. The police stopped him and drove him home. But he got stroppy and my wife, now with a swollen belly, arranged for her brother, in other words my brother-in-law, who incidentally is a man I dislike more actively than most, to ski up here with the sleigh and leave Gregus with me. He wanted to be in the forest with Bongo and me, come hell or high water, and now he's here and he's having a whale of a time. He's never been happier. He helps me with the totem pole and he's so touchingly patient. We've come to the joint decision that he'll be one of the central motifs. He'll have pride of place at the very top. Sitting on top of Bongo. I've already sketched in his outline. I think it's going to turn out fine. Gregus will undoubtedly give the whole some meaning. Three generations of Doppler. Plus Bongo. The totem pole will contain elements of greatness. Our descendants will walk past it and bow their heads in reverence. That was the time when Doppler was Doppler, they'll be thinking. And especially if later generations of Dopplers degenerate in the way that I suspect they will. I will represent a pinnacle in Doppler production. Little old me. And I don't even like people. However, even though parts of me think it's fine that Gregus is here, there is still quite a large part that wants to be alone in the forest, and it's having a hell of a struggle with this new situation.

As if the reactionary hadn't made things complicated enough already.

On top of all this, Düsseldorf has announced his appearance. He skies round here several times a week and occasionally he stays the night. After *Norway Countrywide* featured him in the programme, he's suffered a bit of a downer. He feels he sold himself too cheaply. He feels that his life is imbued with a greater complexity than *Norway Countrywide* managed to get across in the five minutes he was on air. They were not able to sound out the real depths of his fatherless existence. It was no more than a feature story about model-building. Like any other *Norway Countrywide* story about model-building. He was portrayed as a man with a somewhat out of the ordinary hobby.

Poor Düsseldorf. I feel truly sorry for him. I can't bring myself to say that I would prefer to be on my own. I lend him a groundsheet and a woollen blanket and sit up until the early hours listening to him. I talk as well. We exchange experiences,

133

one might say. About being us. Maybe he's the closest thing I will ever have to a kind of friend, even though of course I would have preferred it if he wasn't here.

Those evenings when the reactionary is here, too, are really strange. He goes on about his festival of brotherhood and it's clear from both Düsseldorf's and my face that few things could interest us less. You've missed the boat, I say. Let the people from the various religions be mutually suspicious, blow each other to smithereens and stick to their beliefs. Sit back and think about something else. But the reactionary thinks about this with an earnestness that borders on my daughter's devotion to Tolkien. He's obsessed with the thought of making amends. He's been a superficial pillock, and now he has to dig deep if he's going to put things right again.

And then we play lotto. Gregus is asleep at one edge of the lavvu tent, Bongo and the reactionary dog lie curled up together at the entrance, while the reactionary, Düsseldorf and I sit in the light of the bonfire playing animal lotto. I feel like a teacher on a school trip.

By the way, Bongo and the reactionary dog are under the delusion they're sweethearts. They hang out together all the time and I have the impression they're planning to have children. Bongo appears smitten and distant, and thus far I haven't had the heart to explain to him that the reactionary dog is a dog and not an elk.

And in the midst of all this the totem pole is beginning to take shape. We're working on Dad's arms. They have to be carved separately and fitted into the side of his body. This is a technique I by no means master and I make several mistakes before finally getting them to look passable. My totem father is given some short bird's wing-like arms which would be useless anywhere else but on a totem pole. But in a way his life was like that, too, I think. He was useless in the same way that most of us are, and in many ways he will be shown more to his advantage on a totem pole. It is actually his very uselessness that is being honoured. That's what I'm building a monument to.

Düsseldorf, who was already feeling quite depressed, hits rock bottom when the father of the young man who performs national anthems phones to say he's going to report Düsseldorf to the police if he ever contacts his son again. And he can forget all about the coastal cruise. That's completely out of the question. But no doubt you would have liked that, you old lecher, the agitated father says. My son and you in a cramped cabin surrounded by high mountains and deep fjords. Düsseldorf can't get a word in, and he is completely shattered when he comes up to the tent after this telephone conversation.

It's a cruel, cruel world, I say, when your motives are called into question without any right of reply. When a sincere wish for friendship is mistaken for sordid scheming.

It shouldn't be like that.

But that's how it is, says Düsseldorf.

Yes, I say. People eat each other and that's that.

Why do you say that? asks Düsseldorf.

I don't really know, I say. But the context seemed to fit.

Düsseldorf nods, and quietly repeats it under his breath.

You're right, he says. It fits.

The reactionary wants to be just like me. He probably doesn't realise it himself, but there are powerful forces in him which quite simply want to be me. It's totally absurd, but he has actually begun to carve his own totem pole. The good thing about this is that I don't see so much of him. All I hear is the sound of him chipping away. I think he's been home to fetch some tools, and I fear I'm going to end up borrowing some of them because that's less energy-sapping than sneaking about in reactionary territory at night picking locks to get into garages and tool sheds. The bad side is that it's pathetic.

You're pathetic, I say.

The forest belongs to everyone, he says.

We don't disagree about that, I say, but the way in which you ape me is pathetic. It's a mystery to me why you're not ashamed of yourself. Surely you don't seriously believe that you hit on the idea of building a totem pole all on your own?

As I understand it, you're erecting a totem pole in memory of your father, he says, whereas this is intended to be a peace totem pole, and that's quite different. It's meant to signify how important it is that people from different religions can begin to talk together.

Enjoy, I say.

The reactionary has also intimated that he would be interested in acquiring an elk. Preferably a calf. And preferably one that resembles Bongo. He's even asked if he could buy Bongo. That, of course, is completely out of the question. The likes of Bongo are not for sale at any price, and I've told him that he can stick his filthy lucre, but then he doubles and triples the price to test me. By the end, he was up around the seventy thousand kroner mark. He felt Bongo was worth that. I turned down the offer, obviously, and since then he has been very curt with me. I suppose he feels a little hurt. He's used to money opening doors, so when he sees it closing them, he takes the attitude that the world is against him and this is difficult to swallow.

I can't stay here any longer. I have to move on. But I want to finish the totem pole before I go. You can't stop honouring your father just because soul-searching reactionaries and other disruptive elements start flooding in. I'm going to have to grit my teeth and finish off what I'm doing. After that I'll pack my bags and make my getaway before anyone knows what's going on. I move up a gear. Work double shifts. Gregus tries to keep up, but because of his tender years he needs twice as much sleep as me. And I get most done in the hours when he's asleep. But when he's awake we hit it off fine nonetheless. We talk about all sorts of things and, to be honest, he's no fool, neither with respect to conversation nor carpentry. I'm not going to make any bones about it, he is smart, but I don't give him any direct compliments. He gets the occasional pat on the shoulder with a bit of muted encouragement. I just quietly let him know that I'm pleased with him. And I really am. He's far and away the best thing I've ever had a hand in creating, and as long as all this smartness doesn't catch up with him he's all set to do well in life. Really I ought to keep him up here with me, as down with his mother, sister and other people he'll inevitably embark upon the road to conventionality. He needs me as a counterweight. He badly needs that. I'm thinking a lot about this just now. Weighing up the pros and cons. I have a desperate need to be on my own, but consideration for Gregus is also weighing on my mind. I don't reach a clear conclusion.

And the days pass. It's not just the odd kilo of wood we're chipping off. The chips are flying in all directions and lie like a blanket over the snow which itself lies like a blanket over the ground. Blanket upon blanket. I ought to start writing poetry.

One day, a Sunday it slowly occurs on me, my brother-in-law skis by to see us. He arrives at a time when Gregus, Düsseldorf and I are all busy working on the totem pole. I'm carving and the two others are filing and sanding. And from the other side of a clump of trees we can hear the rhythmic axe blows of the reactionary. My brother-in-law remarks that we seem a pretty cool bunch, and he adds that it's good to see that I'm not so alone any more. As for him, he's covered quite a bit of ground and dropped by several cabins and can report that there are quite a few people on the move outside the city. And, by the way, he says, a message from my wife, she expects Gregus and me to be back down in Oslo by the middle of April, by which she means the 15th. That's when she's due and by that time this farce will have been going on for long enough, he says. His sister is not the kind you can just marry and then do a runner when you feel like it. Other people's sisters maybe, but not his.

I nod.

And if you're not there, I'll come and get you, he says.

No problem, I say.

I can see that my brother-in-law is relieved. He had no doubt expected more resistance. Maybe he had been dreading it, but then everything turns out fine, pleasant almost. The reason for this is that I'm lying. But he doesn't know that. A lie is a splendid device, far too seldom used. It's incredibly effective. You say one thing and you mean something completely different. Fantastic.

When my brother-in-law leaves I stand on the trunk of the totem pole and wave him goodbye in a friendly, brother-in-law-like manner, but as soon as he turns away I pull tiny faces at him, and of course Gregus sees this.

Why did you do that, Dad? he asks.

Do what? I ask.

You did this with your face, he says, mimicking me.

Düsseldorf follows the conversation without saying a word, but I suspect that he's eager to see how I will tackle the situation. I've told him on several occasions how intensely negative my attitude to my brother-in-law is and I've recounted anecdotes about how hopeless our relationship has been over the years.

I got a midge in my eye, I say, but can see Düsseldorf discreetly shaking his head. That one won't wash.

There aren't any midges here, says Gregus. As bloody logical as always.

OK, OK, I say. I did it because I think Uncle Tom is, I hesitate, a bit of a drag. We're very different. We don't really speak the same language. At times he can be alright, such as when he helped me to build the garage, but at other times he's short on grey matter, to put it bluntly. And right now I'm tending to think the latter.

Düsseldorf discreetly nods to applaud my directness.

Got a nice cabin, though, Gregus says.

True enough, I say.

april and may

Things are going progressively downhill around here. Düsseldorf has begun to drink quite heavily. He's shuttling between the *vinmonopol* and the tent. He's got himself a pair of snowshoes. He also brings back food, especially takeaway pizzas, and that helps to buoy the mood. There's not much left of Bongo's mother, and out of consideration for Bongo I don't think I can kill another elk for the time being. I could bag a deer maybe, but they're so bloody shy. And of course there aren't any bears or wolves up here. The authorities have fenced them all in farther east to make it easier for the indigenous population to exterminate them on the quiet.

There has been a lot of snow this winter, but now it's melting away in chunks by the day. When the snow has gone, I'm off. Then nobody will be able to follow my tracks. Then I'll be free.

Gregus has grown tired of the totem pole and spends most of his time inside the tent. Armed with a pile of newspapers for lighting the fire, and a few tips from a drunken Düsseldorf, Gregus has learned to read. Goodness me, it's frightening how this drive to achieve is embedded in the genes. There's no stopping it. It finds its own way. Just like water, it erodes any obstacles in its path and gets to wherever it wants to go. For me this is the last straw. If he can read at the age of four before you know it he's going to be doing quadratic and cubic equations. He has to be stopped. His urge to conform has to be nipped in the bud. Gregus is not going down to civilisation. He's going to stay in the forest with me. And I'm going to start lighting the fire with birch bark. The newspapers will have to be burned right away, so if Gregus wants to do some more reading he will have to write the texts himself. He'll have to carve them in bark or write them in blood. That'll put the skids under his reading pursuits, I reckon.

We don't see much of the reactionary. He's already finished his totem pole. It's an eyesore and very unlikely to be used anywhere on earth to create peace. We helped him to erect it a few days ago. We had to light a fire to thaw the ground under the snow, but somehow we finally got it up. There it stands as a shining monument to the reactionary's failed act of penance and forlorn search. Now he's now gone back to the people to pin posters to notice boards in shops, vegetarian restaurants and on lamp posts, inviting people to come to the festival of brotherhood which is to be held here on 16th and 17th May. Luckily, Gregus and I will not be here at that time. We'll be over the hills and far away by then. So they can form all the brotherhoods they want on their own. Why he's chosen to hold the festival at the same time as

Independence Day I've no idea. The combination of religion and the founding of the Constitution is even more repulsive of course, but I think he should just get on with it. I'm not going to form any brotherhoods with anyone. That's for bloody certain.

To complete the chaos up here, Toolman Roger has also turned up. His girlfriend has kicked him out. She'd had enough of him squirting his sperm all over the place. As ill luck would have it, he squirted over a book that his girlfriend had just unwrapped and was looking forward to reading. That was one squirt too far, and now he's here by the fire drinking with Düsseldorf. They've become pally and Roger is complaining that his girlfriend didn't make her views clear enough. He had begun to sense that perhaps she didn't think all the squirting was so amusing any more, but he didn't get the requisite unambiguous signals for him to stop. Only a few days ago, for example, he had squirted on a bill from the Norwegian Automobile Association, and both of them had had a good laugh at that. So why not a book from the book club? That's women for you, says Roger. It's impossible to know where you stand with them. Something that has been okay for ages is suddenly wrong. It changes from one second to the next.

While the others drink or sleep I carve away at the totem pole for all I'm worth, reflecting that I don't recognise my own

145

forest any more. The forest that was once so quiet and peaceful. Bongo and I were here from morning till night in a kind of harmonious balance, and didn't adapt for anyone. On the contrary, we did just as we pleased. And I was slowly closing in on my goal, which was to do nothing. But that was before. Now there is not much left of the forest I once knew. We must have come to the wrong forest, I say to Bongo. It's so strange here.

One problem with people is that as soon as they fill a space it's them you see and not the space. Large, desolate landscapes stop being large, desolate landscapes once they have people in them. They define what the eye sees. And the human eye is almost always directed at other humans. In this way an illusion is created that humans are more important than those things on earth which are not human. It's a sick illusion. Perhaps elk are the most important creatures when it comes down to it, I say to Bongo. Perhaps you're the ones who know best but you're extremely patient. I doubt that, of course, but who knows? It's definitely not humans anyway. I refuse to believe that.

Things take their unusual course and the snow disappears. Gregus reads, Roger and Düsseldorf drink themselves stupid, the reactionary hangs up his brotherhood notices in vegetarian restaurants and I put the finishing touches to my painstakingly crafted totem pole. The intricate detail is beginning to stand out, and I can see that I've created a fine piece of work. This is something of which I can be proud. Any idiot will be able to see that the totem pole depicts a man sitting on an egg, with another man on his head, sitting on a bike, and that this other man has a year-old elk on his head and on this elk sits a little boy. It's figurative to the nth degree but at the same time stylised so as not to reveal our actual identities. Now it has to be rubbed down with sandpaper and painted in bright colours. I'll avoid making the same blunder that the North American West Coast Indians always made. They carved their fantastic totem poles and stood them in the ground without treating them in any way. Consequently they lasted only a few decades before nature reclaimed them. They simply fell and rotted away. Which was completely in keeping with the Indians' beliefs in wholeness and cycles and all that kind of thing. Earth to earth etc. I suppose my thinking differs here from the Indians. After all, I am not an Indian, but a man of my time. A failed man of my time. Or just a man of a failed time. Depending on how you look at it. Either way, I want to make a thorough job of it. I'm going to give it the works with several coats of creosote and woodstain and then paint it in bright colours capable of withstanding the Norwegian winter. It should definitely be able to last a thousand years. Minimum. A thousand sounds good. That's the optimum number.

One quiet spring night I make my way down to Ullevaal Stadium and smash the window of the ironmonger's shop.

 147

I'm sure I could have got the money from Düsseldorf, but he's drunk and fatherless all the time these days, and not only that, I like the idea of making a totem pole for nothing. I like everything that doesn't cost money. I'm immediately on my guard if projects come with a budget. That's how it is now. I've changed. I'll soon have been in the forest for a whole year and I'm not the person I was. It's not easy to say when the change occurred. It most likely came about gradually, as most changes do, but the fact that something has happened is beyond doubt. The forest gives and it takes. And it shapes those who take refuge there in its own image. I'm in the process of becoming a forest myself. The forest, that's me, I think, as I'm met by the infernal sound of the alarm and calmly calculate that I have about five minutes to do the job. I carry out pot after pot of paint and lacquer and woodstain and whatever else I can lay my hands on. I run as fast as I can and after five minutes I've managed to hide a considerable amount of paint products behind the same skip that the ICA manager has been putting my milk behind for some months now. When I reckon I have what I need, I crouch down on top of all the pots and wait for Securitas to come. At length, a guard appears, but much later than I had thought. And the police turn up and there's quite a lot of note-taking and phoning, and finally the shopkeeper himself arrives. I recognise him from the countless small purchases I made in connection with our endless redecorating. A paintbrush here, bit of tape there, sunflower seeds for the birds. I've always been a man for the birds. They have a lot to thank me for, the birds do, and I've been on nodding terms with this shopkeeper for years, but now I've taken the step of smashing the window in his shop and helping myself to what I need. That kind of thing should come as no surprise to him. It's part and parcel of having a shop. He patches up the window with some Plexiglass-like material and eventually leaves. I have a couple of hours before the locals wake up, and I take Bongo to the edge of the forest and load him up with inhuman amounts of woodstain and paint, and it takes us three round trips to get all the goods back home.

On May 1st, the reactionary returns. And to provoke me he has brought along a bin bag full of old leaves, which he proceeds to burn outside his tent, standing there with a rake he pokes in the bonfire while it's burning. I ignore him. I haven't time to do anything else. I don't even take time off to celebrate International Workers' Day. I have more important things to do. And, as a matter of fact, who are the workers in Norway today? Damned if I know. So I paint. The egg shaker becomes fire-engine red, and Dad is given a variety of colours on his upper and lower body. I feel he deserves that. I myself go green, like the forest, and I paint the bike in extremely realistic colours, using my own bike as the model. Bongo goes yellow and Gregus a sort of turquoise. Individual features on the faces, such as eyes, mouth and nose, are painted in contrasting colours. I coat the plinth with everything that is

149

left. It probably gets twenty coats of all sorts of weird and wonderful things, and I doubt whether a thousand years of moisture will make any inroads.

As I paint, Gregus irritates me by spelling his way through old newspaper articles about all kinds of rubbish. Politics and science and art and culture. And not only does he painstakingly read them out, letter by letter, but he tries to analyse the content, to the best of his meagre abilities, and is eager to discuss what it means. Forget it, I say. It means nothing. It's just words. It must mean something, Gregus says. Nope, I say. People just write things to show how smart they are, and that's the last thing the world needs. It's just words, words, words. Maybe a small percentage of it is slightly more than words, but to know which bit you have to be smarter than most and I forbid you to have that as your goal at such an early stage in your life.

I don't believe it doesn't mean anything, says Gregus.

What you do when you come of age is none of my business, I say. I promise to release my hold over you when that time comes. But that's many years in the future. And the only thing that matters right now is this totem pole. It's going to stand for a thousand years and bear witness to the fact that you and I and Grandad and Bongo have been here. We have been on earth. We have had our time and did our best and even so were useless in a useless way, and when it's finished you and I are going to head off, I say. And the newspaper articles aren't coming with us. You can just forget all about your reading project. And the same goes for school. You're not going to get a sniff of school until you're eighteen. We're going to be in the forest, I say. With Bongo. You might as well get used to the idea right now.

I can make my own decisions, can't I? he says.

Forget it, I say.

But there's something here about a school called the London School of something, yes, here it is, London School of Economics, says Gregus. Isn't that where Peter Pan comes from?

That's right, I say.

I bet it's great going to school there, he says.

Bear in mind that if you ever start at that school I'll come and live in the forest outside London and give you a good hiding every single day.

But I'll be allowed to live in London, won't I? says Gregus.

Yes, of course, I say. It's an exhilarating city. But you can just hang around there a bit, can't you? Or go to a school that isn't so nice and conventional? Maybe something arty? A school that gives you the skills to extend boundaries rather than maintain them?

I don't understand what you're talking about, says Gregus.

You're lucky, I say.

And thanks to this meaningless conversation I go around singing the 'I Can Fly' song from the *Peter Pan* film for days. As I paint I hum the tune and sing the chorus, and I do it hundreds of times and in the end I feel genuinely sorry that I can't fly.

The totem pole is finished.

In the final stages I use the confiscated head lamp and work around the clock. The very last thing I do is to paint a large sexual organ on my father. I give him the Doppler family hallmark. After that I take a few steps back and can see that the result is fantastic. It has become a totem pole the like of which the world has never seen. It is deeply meaningful and personal, and it's colourful, if not garish. It's uplifting. And I, Doppler, I made it. With my own hands. I have honoured my father in a way he would never have imagined possible, and I have felt close to him.

As soon as it's finished I set about digging a hole in the ground. I choose a spot down by the pissing place. From there, as I've already mentioned, you can see large tracts of Oslo, and a bit of piss won't do any harm, I think. On the contrary. It is, as I see it, recognition of the fact that my father took pictures of toilets in his later years. Granted, he never pissed here. But he definitely would have done if he'd had the chance. Pissing against the totem pole will be like consecrating the family bonds, I think. Doppler piss is as thick as blood, more or less, and it binds us together. Later generations of Dopplers will make pilgrimages to this place to pay their respects to earlier Dopplers by pissing on the family totem pole.

But half a metre down I hit bedrock. There's so much bedrock in this bloody country of ours that I can't even be bothered to make jokes about it. Suffice it to say there's enough bedrock for everyone and this virtually encyclopaedic fact blows my schedule to smithereens. I had envisaged that Gregus and Bongo and I would be miles away by the middle of May, and my brother-in-law would have had to return empty-handed when he came to fetch me, but now I'm not so sure any more. Maybe I'll have to stay here and fight. In that case I'll have to let fly with an arrow just as I did with the reactionary. That would serve him right, that's for sure, but it would jeopardise my escape plans and I'd prefer not to do that.

For two weeks I have a bonfire going constantly in the hole and pour water down to get the rock to crack. Bonfire after bonfire. I spend the days chopping wood and carrying water. Gregus helps me, but the others booze and are a dead loss. Fair enough. I've no intention of trying to making them see the error of their ways. If they want to drink, that's their business. I've been alive long enough to know that there are umpteen reasons for drinking yourself silly and everyone has to do what they think best. The reactionary doesn't drink. Let that be said. He's working hammer and tongs in the forest somewhere. He's taking the brotherhood festival seriously. No doubt about that. He's making benches and tables and a small stage where I presume he's going to stand and talk about peace on earth and reconciliation between peoples of

153

the world.

It's difficult to say where one bonfire ends and a new one begins, but after forty or fifty of them I've made a hole of a metre or so down into the rock, and after just as many more fires I'm getting close to two metres. That's good. But it's May now, indeed it's almost the middle of May. The snow has gone and the forest is dry. White and blue anemones are flowering everywhere and a new generation of elk is on its way all over the forest. You're not the youngest any more, I say to Bongo, and you may think that obliges you to grow up fast, but you shouldn't think like that. I think you should hold on to your youthful freedom and independence. Do crazy things. Have a party. Be a stirrer and raise hell. This is me Doppler saying this, I say. And Doppler was possibly one of the most conformist yuppies in the country at one time. Now he's retired and works more on a free-lance basis. As a consultant, you might say. To himself and to those who care to listen. There are not so many of them, it seems.

We can't lift the totem pole. Even with the reactionary lending a reluctant hand we don't stand a chance. The damned thing weighs too much. Bongo and I managed to drag it through the snow, but four men, a child and an elk can't lift it into the hole.

How many people do you think will be coming to the brotherhood festival? I ask the reactionary.

Thirty or forty maybe, he says.

Would you mind if I used them? I ask.

I suppose not, he says. It might bring them together.

Exactly, I say. You can't beat symbolically-laden hard graft for uniting people.

The middle of May comes and goes. I sit all day with my bow drawn, listening for my brother-in-law's fleet footfalls, but he fails to appear, and the only reason he fails to appear must be that the birth is overdue. That's perfect. The forces of nature are on my side, but I don't attribute that to fate. It's sheer good luck. Chance is my friend today, and I use the opportunity to enjoy a small glass with Düsseldorf and Roger. At night I sleep with my bow and arrow under my pillow, but fortunately I see nothing of my brother-in-law, neither in my dreams nor in so-called reality.

*

Next morning the brotherhood festival begins. The reactionary has adorned himself in something as unreactionary as a workman's smock. Maybe he feels it makes it easier for him to step into a different sphere, a more elevated spirituality, I don't know, he's standing there anyway, ready to receive good people from all the religions of the world, but they're not exactly arriving in droves. Four or five hours after the festival should have started he's forced to acknowledge that there are only four takers for the festival. A Muslim has turned up, as well as a Jew, a Christian and a journalist from the evening edition of *Aftenposten*. All four of them are sitting on a log waiting for the

 155

reactionary to say something. At long last, he steps forward and declares the festival open. He is unable to conceal his disappointment, but nonetheless reels off some fairly credible phrases about each individual, in such troubled times as ours, having to look inside ourselves to examine how deep our tolerance runs etc. We must understand one another, and the key to understanding lies in knowing one another. Quite simply, we need to learn more about each other. We need to know what others think and believe and fear, but also more commonplace things, such as what time they get up in the morning, and what they have for dinner. Everything is useful. In truth we can never learn too much about each other. And these two days are to be spent doing just that. We will exchange information about everything under the sun. The three believers nod and the journalist takes notes.

The first exercise is to let yourself fall backwards hoping and trusting that the others will catch hold of you. There are so few of us that this presents some problems. The burly Muslim hits the ground a couple of times, but is soon up on his feet, insisting that it's his own fault. All the rest of us land safely in others' outstretched arms. Actually, it gives me a certain amount of pleasure. I fall back, lose control and for a split second find myself between heaven and earth, and then instead of hitting the ground with a bang I am caught by the soft and tender arms of my fellow man.

The next item on the programme is to form pairs and blindfold one of the partners and then guide him around the vicinity. The blind partner has to learn to rely on the sighted person. It's a great little exercise from which we all learn something, even though Bongo, who I team up with, once again demonstrates to all and sundry that he's a bit slower on the uptake than the rest of us when it comes to getting the gist of a very clear message. As we pass the Jew and the *Aftenposten* journalist, I notice that the latter is crying while walking along blindfolded. It must be a bit too much for him, I suppose. He's used to verbal flights of fancy and here it's suddenly physicality that's in the ascendancy, and there's intimacy and other unfamiliar things. It can soon become too much. And of course the wily old foxes on the editorial staff may have made sure they wriggled out of an assignment like this, and instead conspired to send the young trainee with the frayed nerves.

The third exercise is, after some coercion from me, to raise the totem pole. Everything is prepared beforehand, and with a concerted effort we force the totem pole into place. It's child's play, or as good as. The monster is carried to the hole and is then slowly shoved and pulled up into an upright position with the aid of an ingenious system of ropes. After that, the festival continues without me.

As Gregus and I hammer wedges into the ground around the totem pole, I can hear that the brotherhood process in the forest is becoming more intense. There's some sort of group work going on. The reactionary's irritated voice rings out from time to time, but I don't feel it has anything to do with me. A festival like this is a praiseworthy initiative, no doubt about that, and the idea is spot on: nations and religions of the world need a helping hand if we're to get out of the pickle we're in. Nobody will be happier than me if they succeed. But I have to admit that I don't have any confidence in it happening. I think we've missed the boat. I believe that those of us who are alive today are destined to die out and will be replaced by a new species of humans. Who will start with a clean sheet and fewer aggressive traits. A more good-natured species of humans. A variant which has the ability to be more liberal.

Eventually the totem pole is positioned just as I want it. It's wedged into place and I've filled the hole around the wedges with small stones, earth and peat. It towers up in the air, spreading colour and the spirit of Doppler around the forest.

It looks really good, in fact, even though I say so myself. I have now settled my differences with my father, I feel. Now he can rest in peace, as they say. And I can have peace of mind because I know that he is resting in peace. Someone has remembered him. One of those closest to him has remembered him and crafted a work of art in his honour. Surely that must warm the cockles of the old rascal's heart. The man who managed to live his whole life without revealing his true identity. I've honoured him and can now set my sights on new horizons. I gather my closest companions around me, Gregus and Bongo that is, and tell them that the time has come to move on. The current state of affairs in the forest is no longer of such a character that we can flourish here, I say. We need air in which to breathe and space in which to formulate grand ideas. The world awaits, I say. We are about to embark on a journey and may be gone for some time. I don't quite know where all this comes from, but I feel it's urgent, so I just come out with it, even though I hadn't really envisaged doing anything once the totem pole was finished. On the contrary, I had intended to do less than any human before me had done. I was going to close in on the magical zero. But now here I am with my two disciples, for I sense that I've begun to consider them as disciples, holding out the prospect of a journey that might well be protracted. Are you prepared for such a journey? I ask them. Gregus nods and Bongo looks at me in the same inscrutable way he always does, but of course I know him inside out and I'm sure that he, like any other teenager, is ready for anything that is fun.

But it's not certain that it will be such fun, I say. We'll see. But not everything can be fun in any case. It's amazing that I'm saying this. It's as if someone else is talking through me. And sometimes you have to do things even though they aren't fun, I say. You have to venture out farther on the branch on which you're sitting, and once in a while you also have to saw it off.

Otherwise you're just a little shitty pants, says Gregus.

Absolutely, I say. Otherwise you're just a little shitty pants.

But where are we going? Gregus asks.

 159

We're going from forest to forest, I say. We'll go into the middle of this forest and eventually maybe come out on the other side. And into the next one. And we can keep on doing that until we know we've had enough. But I doubt whether we'll have had enough after the first one.

There are always more forests.

I tell them that now we should all piss on the totem pole and after that get ourselves ready so we can quietly dismantle the tent during the night and be over the hills and far away before the others wake up in the morning.

We all piss and allow our streams to cross in honour of our father and grandfather, who will stand here for a thousand years.

The countdown has begun.

*

As we pack, the brotherhood festival is getting into full swing. They're singing and hollering out there and it's obvious that Düsseldorf and Roger have provided alcohol for the festival. This is hardly what the reactionary had in mind, but why not, I think, as I work the tent pegs loose. Alcohol will probably loosen them up a bit and they might well get to know each other better that way than they otherwise would have done. As spirits in the neighbouring camp get higher, I realise that there is no longer any rush to take down the tent. They have already reached a point where their awareness of the outside world is so minimal that I can operate without fear of being disturbed.

I make a sled from two birch trees that Bongo can tow. Onto this I load the tent, tools and actually most of my worldly goods in the forest. I take the axes along with me. The farmer will have to get himself some new ones. Maybe there aren't many axes where we're going.

I pack all night, while Bongo and Gregus sleep side by side.

Early the next morning I stroll over to the festival-goers to say goodbye. The Christian has been asleep in a strange, drunken position, and the representatives of the two other world religions are in the process of squeezing toothpaste under his foreskin. They are roaring with laughter and having the time of their lives. The reactionary is sitting by a fire telling the *Aftenposten* journalist, who if possible is drunker than any of the others, that he wished his wife's breasts were more like boats. The journalist can barely hold the pen he is taking notes with. What do you mean by that? he asks. Boat-like, says the reactionary. More like boats. Düsseldorf and Roger are the most experienced drinkers and are therefore the most active at this point. I shake them by the hand and say that I'm pleased to have met them but now I'm setting out on a journey which might be lengthy. Take care of yourselves, I wish them. You, too, they say, whereafter they settle back down in the heather and carry on with a conversation the subject of which is unknown to me. As is the case with most other conversations on this earth. There are very few I take part in myself. I have no idea what all the other billions of conversations are about. And a good job, too.

Independence Day is already well under way when at long last we're ready to leave. We can hear the drone of various brass bands coming from down amongst the people. Let them, if that's what they want, I think as I fasten the sled around Bongo's neck. Then my brother-in-law appears. He would, wouldn't he. He glides up to me in that irritating, fleet-footed manner of his, rifle over shoulder. He's come prepared to shoot me. Christ. I run in amongst the trees and fumble about trying to place an arrow on the bowstring. Stop! I hear my brother-in-law shout, whereupon I let fly an arrow in the direction the sound came from. I run this way and that, zigzagging, but my brother-in-law is fresh after a good night's sleep and he soon collars me. He wastes no time and summarily shoots me in the leg with a tranquiliser dart. I can see the dart lodged in my calf. It looks just like all the other darts of this type I've seen on TV when zoologists have to anaesthetise animals on the African steppes or wolves in the Norwegian-Swedish borderland. All of a sudden my body feels heavy and I sink gently into the heather. It's a fantastically beautiful day, I have time to reflect. The birch trees are a mass of green with their newly sprung buds and it's Independence Day in the forest. Everything is pure. Everything is Norwegian.

I am semi-conscious in an odd, uncomfortable way as my brother-in-law carries me in a fireman's lift down to the Rikshospital. Gregus and Bongo tag along behind. The streets are full of festively dressed people everywhere. I detest 17th May, I think in a sedated sort of way. I have never quite realised before how much I detest this day, but now I do. I detest this way of celebrating all things Norwegian. And I detest all those national costumes. Each one uglier than the next. And just when I think I've seen the ugliest of the lot, bugger me if somebody doesn't come along in an even uglier one.

My brother-in-law carries me straight into the Rikshospital. Into the lift. And up. And into a room where my wife is lying with a little boy on her stomach. My boy. Or ours, as they say nowadays. As of course they should. Bonny boy, I say, and hold him for a bit. On somewhat shaky legs I carry him over to the window and quietly whisper in his ear that I'm going with his brother on a journey that might be protracted, but I'll see him again some time. In a few years maybe. And that he should take care of himself in the meantime. Don't toe the line, I say. It's okay to pretend to be listening to what your mother says, but do the opposite. If you always do the opposite, things will turn out fine. Promise me that. Do whatever you want, but keep away from conformity.

While my wife is talking to Gregus and Nora, who has also arrived, I feel my strength returning, as well as a good deal of aggression, and I force my brother-in-law down onto the floor and tie him to the sink with a sheet. You're not so tough any more now, are you, I say. You're tied to the sink. You're not going anywhere. What do you think of that, eh? He strains at the sheet like a taunted beast of prey. And I'm not the kind of person to allow himself to be shot with a tranquiliser dart so you can examine him or have him do your will. I'm not going to let anyone examine me, and I won't be subjected to anyone else's will. Understand?

He nods.

And if you ever shoot me again, that'll be the last thing you do.

He nods again.

I pat the little one and tell my wife it's great to see him. Was the birth okay? I ask.

It was fine, she says. The best so far. I was thinking of calling him Bjørnstjerne, after Bjørnstjerne Bjørnson, the Nobel prizewinner, she says. I mean, since he was born today, you know.

I just knew it, I think, putting on a forced warm smile. My wife's oh so nice conformity knows no bounds. It's disgusting that we're going to fill this little lad with so much Norwegianness on the very first day of his life, but, when you think of it, most of what we do is disgusting, so I'm not going to let it bother me for now.

By the way, I want to have even more children, says my wife.

Steady on, I say. Maybe we can have more children some

time, but I still have unfinished business in the forest. Both in this forest and in others, and I have to travel the world a bit and won't be back for a good while. And nor will Gregus.

My wife eyes Gregus, who nods.

We're going on a journey, I say. And we might be gone a long time.

Where are you going? My wife asks.

From forest to forest, I say. In a way, it's a calling. Things are happening out there and we're needed.

My wife looks at me in wonderment.

It's something we have to do, I say. Something important.

Can you be more specific? my wife asks.

No, I say. I can be less specific. But not more. All I know is that we have to get moving because the forest is calling us.

Calling you? says my wife.

That's exactly what it's doing, I say. For there are other lives than the life we've lived for many years now, I say. There are other things besides Smart Club and children's birthdays and dinner with so-called friends and our repulsively Norwegian notion of social cosiness, which allows us to be both the most affable and the most self-centered nation in the world.

What other life? asks my wife.

That's what I have to find out about, I say. And when I find the answer, I'll tell you.

Is this what you want, Gregus? My wife asks.

Gregus nods.

165

Do as you wish, my wife says. I don't understand one iota of it, but if you're called, then you're called. That much I do understand.

It occurs to me that it must be the painkillers she was given for the birth that have made her tolerant and magnanimous, and we use the chance to make our escape.

On our way out we say a quick goodbye to Bjørnstjerne, my wife and her brother, who is still bound to the sink in a way which is unfathomable to him. When we are about to take our leave of Nora she solemnly shakes my hand and mumbles something in what I assume must be Elvish. Presumably she's so far into Tolkien's world that she instinctively begins to think on a grand scale when people set out on long journeys. My Elvish isn't up to much, but I suspect that she's showering us with good wishes, and hopes that we'll finally manage to throw the perfidious ring, or whatever it is we're battling with, into some volcano.

We find Bongo grazing behind the hospital, and side by side the three of us wade across the stream leading to Lake Sognvann and allow ourselves to be swallowed up by the forest. We walk northwards for the first few hours after which we turn and proceed in a more easterly direction. We walk along in silence. Stopping occasionally to share a bit of Düsseldorf's Toblerone, of which there are still two or three kilos left and which, incidentally, is the only thing we have resembling food. Towards evening Gregus falls asleep and is allowed to rest on Bongo's sled, and as we move farther into the forest I breathe more easily. Out here, there aren't any national costumes, nor is there an Independence Day. There's only forest. As there was only forest the day I fell off my bike; as there was until the reactionary turned up with all that messy soul-searching of his, and those Løvenskiold threats. Fuck Løvenskiold, by the way. In a few hours we'll be out of his jurisdiction. He can keep his rotten forest. Where we're going he won't be able to lay his hands on us however hard he tries. We're going to bigger forests than he has ever heard of. And the best thing of all is, I'm alone again. With two disciples, it has to be said, but alone nevertheless. Always alone. Like elk. Like my father.

I think about two things as I walk along.

The first is about my not liking people. I still don't. But I've begun to see that I need to be sufficiently open-minded to admit that this is based on my knowledge of those around me, people in Norway, that is, or Norwegians as they're also called. I've drawn my fairly dramatic conclusions on the basis of them. And of course that won't do. I have to meet others. I have to open my mind to the fact that somewhere out there it might be possible to find intelligent life that stands for something else. I will wander on until I meet this other form of life. Or until I have established with incontrovertible evidence that it doesn't exist.

The other thing I think about is that this is a military campaign. We're going on a military campaign. It's no good fooling around in the secure Norwegian forest any more. I've had closure with my father and now I have to raise my sights, it's onwards and upwards unless I want to drown in my own emptiness. Outside this country lies a whole world I don't know. And it needs help. It needs the help of a hunter-gatherer like me, like Chopper Doppler, not to mince my words. And an elk like Bongo. And maybe also a young lad like Gregus. Living in Norway doesn't give you a true picture of things, I think. Norway has a thousand billion kroner in the bank. It sounds like a make-believe figure. Like a figure you would pluck from the air to exemplify an enormous amount of something. But the figure is real. Norway is good for a thousand billion kroner. Oil has given us this money. Every time conflicts around the world push the price of oil up, we're raking the money in. And there are so few of us. And who owns the oil at the bottom of the sea and the hydro-electric power in the rivers? one might wonder, while we're on the subject. And how can we buy or sell anything at all? For Norway is an insignificant suburb in the real world. And we're in the process of distancing ourselves farther and farther from it. And these thoughts are smart, I muse, but what the hell. So be it, if they also serve a purpose.

Our little procession is on its way out of Norway to the rest of the world. We're going east. We're going to hunt and gather our way to other people. Whom I may or may not like any better than those who live here. We shall see.

This is a military campaign. We are soldiers and we're

going to fight to the last man.

Against smartness. Against stupidity.

Because it's war out there.

It's war.

To be continued

(inshallah)